One Night One Day

A play in two-acts by Martin Lindsay

Moody Lapcat Books

First paperback edition in 2025.

Design and Cover by Martin Lindsay.

Images by Mike McAllan, Martin Lindsay and Canva.

ISBN: 978-0-6451987-8-2 (paperback)

ISBN: 978-0-6451987-9-9 (ebook)

Published by Moody Lapcat Books

Perth, Western Australia

www.moodylapcatbooks.com

contact@moodylapcatbooks.com

Characters

RACHEL—20s to 40s

"I've kissed enough frogs to know they just stay frogs. Or turn into toads."

> Jaded and weary, Rachel uses sarcasm as a self-preservation strategy, pre-emptively pushing people away by default. She is often left to fix messes left by her careless—but carefree—drunken self.

GREG—20s to 40s

"Look on the bright side. You got laid last night! And you know what? So did I! What a great day to be alive!"

> A goofy bravado hides Greg's self-doubts about his less than successful love life. Impulsively chases opportunities with a goldfish's consideration of consequences but is an awkward romantic at heart.

BOB—40s to 60s

"The stories people tell me. So sad. And after I've had a few—quite a few—I sometimes sort of ... help things along a little."

> A dishevelled public servant who has stagnated within his position of authority. Despite an unhappy marriage, Bob is jolly and soft-hearted—fond of a drink, a dirty joke, and a sing song.

JANE—20s to 30s

"You really need to stop inviting strange old men into our house. At the very least, that particular one out there."

An attractive energetic young woman, prone to excitedly bursting into rooms. Focus isn't one of her strengths. Jane has a rosy view of the future, with plans for a perfect marriage that escalate to bridezilla proportions.

Setting

The entire play is set in Rachel's bedroom.

Rachel's bedroom consists of:

- BED with PILLOWS and SHEET, with BEDSIDE TABLE on RACHEL's side.

- DRESSER with MIRROR and CHAIR.

- DOOR to side of stage.

For Act 1, the set should be pre-dressed:

- Lots of CLOTHES scattered across floor.

- TRAFFIC CONES, GNOMES etc under BED.

- DOONA at foot of bed concealing BOB.

- WINE GLASS on RACHEL's BEDSIDE TABLE.

- RACHEL's MOBILE PHONE on BEDSIDE TABLE.

- LAMP on BEDSIDE TABLE, with BRA laid across it.

- CAR KEYS hidden somewhere on stage for JANE to find, and GREG to never happen upon.

- GREG's BOXERS, JEANS, SHIRT on floor at his side of BED. Also, RACHEL's KNICKERS.

- MARRIAGE CERTIFICATE in GREG's JEANS pocket.

- RACHEL's PYJAMAS within arm's reach on floor by RACHEL's side of the BED.

For Act 2, the set should be pre-dressed:

- Lots of CLOTHES scattered across floor.
- BRIDESMAID DRESS hanging over CLOTHES RACK.
- DOONA and SHEET on BED.

Production Notes

Introductory music can be synched in as Rachel's Mobile phone ringtone at the start of the play.

Ensure the bed sheet is non-see-through under stage lights. Thread count is the nude actor's friend.

Rachel is pre-dressed with bra and pyjama bottoms under sheet at commencement.

The Bedroom door will need to be solidly secured for the various comings and goings.

Mobile message and call cues are best done using a sound effect and actor reactions towards the relevant phone, rather than timing live calls.

In Act 2, either Greg's MOBILE or his JEANS could have a means or mechanism for his JEANS to "vibrate" on the stage floor.

First Performed

Originally performed as the one-act *"One Night Stand Off"*.

Garrick Theatre, Perth, Western Australia, 2008.

Directed by Danni Ashton and Martin Lindsay.

Original Cast

- Rachel—Jayma Knudson
- Greg—Martin Lindsay
- Bob—Graeme Sharp
- Jane—Gemma Sharp

Winner 2008 Southwest Drama Festival Best Play (Western Australia).

Winner 2008 Southwest Drama Festival Best Script (Western Australia).

Winner 2008 Dramafest Festival Best Script (Western Australia).

Original performance of the two-act *"One Night One Day"*.

Blak Yak Theatre, Perth, Western Australia, 2020.

Directed by Melissa Merchant.

Original Cast

- Rachel—Sjaan Lucas
- Greg—Joel Sammels
- Bob—Jarrod Buttery
- Jane—Ellin Sears

ACT ONE

Double BED with PILLOWS is occupied by GREG and RACHEL, asleep and naked under SHEET.

CLOTHES are strewn about—they clearly undressed in a hurry. The rest is RACHEL's general messiness.

DOONA is a large lump at the foot of BED.

On BEDSIDE TABLE next to RACHEL, MOBILE is ringing.

SOUND FX: RACHEL'S MOBILE RINGTONE.

LIGHTS up.

The caller giving up, the MOBILE stops ringing, followed by …

SOUND FX: RACHEL'S MOBILE SMS BEEP.

GREG sits up with a start, swiftly followed by his hangover. He scans the strange surroundings, wondering where he has ended up, until …

GREG discovers RACHEL asleep next to him. Realising, he beams a smile at his success. Warily, he lifts SHEET for a peek …

SOUND FX: RACHEL'S MOBILE SMS BEEP.

GREG immediately pretends to be asleep.

RACHEL drowsily sits up and groans at MOBILE.

RACHEL

Ugh. Bugger off.

RACHEL flops back into PILLOW.

A beat. RACHEL sits up in surprise staring at the stranger next to her. She winces for the situation and her headache kicking in.

Curiosity strikes—she slowly lifts SHEET for a peek…

…GREG instantly snatches SHEET to cover himself.

GREG

Hey!

RACHEL

Sorry.

GREG

… I *was* asleep just then.

Suspicious of his honesty, RACHEL pulls SHEET round herself.

GREG defensively grabs enough SHEET for coverage.

Locked in territorial dispute, hangovers lingering, GREG and RACHEL remain wary of the other's next move.

GREG

So … good morning.

RACHEL

Morning.

Unsure, GREG leans across to kiss her cheek. RACHEL shies.

RACHEL

What are you doing?

GREG

I dunno, really. What do you normally do in situations like this?

RACHEL

I don't *normally* have situations like this.

GREG

No. I'm sure you don't.

RACHEL

Obviously, I could if I wanted to.

GREG

Obviously. And obviously you wanted to with me last night.

RACHEL

That's less obvious. But I don't normally do *this* on a regular basis. Semi-regular, at most. *Occasionally* even. Not that there's anything wrong if it was often—not that it was—as it's my choice and not something to feel guilty about if I did. Only I didn't. And I don't. Not *often* anyway. A *normal* number of times. Statistically speaking.

GREG stares blankly, having lost track long ago.

GREG

... okay.

RACHEL

Do you? "Normally"?

GREG

Hardly ever. More's the pity.

No appropriate words spring to hungover minds.

GREG

A bit embarrassing but I can't recall your name.

RACHEL

(Unimpressed) Rachel.

GREG

Right. Sorry, I ... sorry.

RACHEL grows uneasy.

RACHEL

I don't know yours either.

GREG

Greg. *(Offers hand)* Pleased to meet you, Rachel.

RACHEL begrudgingly shakes.

They lie back, still nursing aching heads.

GREG

Do you remember anything of last night at all?

They grasp at fragmented memories.

RACHEL

We met at the pub. La Parisienne.

GREG

I think I was at The Crown and Badger.

RACHEL

How did I end up there?

GREG

How did I? I thought I was barred.

RACHEL

(Holding head) I wish I had been.

GREG

Anyway, it looks like we hit it off.

RACHEL grimaces at his understatement, then relents.

RACHEL

Sorry, morning isn't my best time of day.

GREG

Yeah, I noticed.

RACHEL reacts, offended.

GREG

Not that I mean you're ... Just that you seem ...
I dunno ... Not that your hair's all crazy.

RACHEL instantly tends her bed hair, paranoid.

GREG

No, it's not. Well, it is. I just meant ... I should
just go, shouldn't I?

RACHEL

You should. Then we forget this ever happened.

GREG

We already have, haven't we?

GREG begins climbing out of BED.

RACHEL

Quietly! Things are bad enough without waking
my housemate and explaining you to her.

GREG

(Turns back, interested) Her?

RACHEL *glares.*

GREG

Just going.

GREG stands, clutching SHEET to cover himself. RACHEL grips her end to avoid being unveiled.

GREG tugs his way. RACHEL determinedly tugs back.

Stalemate, the SHEET held taut between them.

GREG grabs PILLOW to cover himself, lets SHEET go. He scans the room, locating his BOXERS on floor.

RACHEL is watching. GREG glares a "do you mind?".

RACHEL shrugs and keeps watching.

GREG tries scooping BOXERS with his feet, without success.

No other resort, GREG bends over to grab BOXERS, clutching PILLOW. RACHEL recoils from what she sees.

Mission accomplished, GREG considers logistics of donning BOXERS while concealing with PILLOW. RACHEL resumes watching.

Carefully, GREG steps into BOXERS, pulls them over PILLOW, then withdraws PILLOW. He strikes a victory pose for RACHEL's benefit. She is less than impressed.

He sniffs PILLOW, grimaces, then tosses it back onto BED.

SOUND FX: RACHEL'S MOBILE SMS BEEP.

RACHEL retrieves MOBILE to check messages. GREG locates his JEANS and continues to dress.

RACHEL
It's been going off all morning.

GREG
Sorry. Had a curry last night.

RACHEL
My phone.

RACHEL ruffles SHEET for odours, then frowns at MOBILE.

RACHEL
"Tell me you're kidding. ROTFL."

GREG
Rolling on the floor laughing.

RACHEL
I know what it means. I'm confused why she is.

GREG
Poor sense of balance?

RACHEL scrolls MOBILE, while GREG dons SHIRT from floor. He notices KNICKERS, slyly grabbing them as conversation continues.

RACHEL

It's one huge conversation thread from seemingly everyone I know. "Yeah, right!". Right what?

GREG

Sounds like you have weird friends.

RACHEL

They couldn't all have sent drunken messages through the night.

GREG

Maybe you sent out some drunken message and they're all responding. You were pretty pickled.

RACHEL looks up to appraise him critically. GREG whirls round innocently, covertly stuffing KNICKERS in pocket.

RACHEL

I certainly was.

SOUND FX: RACHEL'S MOBILE SMS BEEP.

RACHEL

(Frustrated) It goes back to the end when a new one comes in! "When when when? Ha ha ha." *(Exasperated at MOBILE)* What what what?

GREG tidies himself in DRESSER MIRROR. RACHEL laboriously scrolls MOBILE.

GREG

Maybe you were boasting about the *hunk* you
were taking home.

RACHEL

Sure. Who wouldn't tell the world they'd picked
up some random at the pub again.

GREG

Again?

RACHEL

At all.

GREG raises eyebrow. RACHEL resumes scrolling.

GREG

You probably couldn't control yourself.

GREG poses in MIRROR.

GREG

"Picked me up *such* a hot guy! Piercing eyes,
rippling muscles, manly stubble." Oh, pimple.

GREG leans forward, squeezes cheek.

GREG

Eww. Sorry.

GREG wipes MIRROR from subsequent mess.

RACHEL

So how did I end up coming home with you instead?

GREG

You felt compelled to tell everyone how lucky you'd struck.

RACHEL

Or complaining about the annoying git pestering me at the pub.

GREG

"So, I slept with him. That'll put him off the scent."

RACHEL

Who's *still* pestering me the next day.

Taking the hint, GREG pats his pockets, then scans the room.

GREG

You seen my keys?

RACHEL

Of course I haven't.

GREG

Can you see anything in this mess?

RACHEL

I've seen more than enough of you.

GREG gets on all fours—his head aches from the change in altitude—then searches among scattered CLOTHES.

SOUND FX: RACHEL'S MOBILE SMS BEEP.

RACHEL

For fuck's sake. *(Laboriously scrolls MOBILE)*

GREG

Just an occasional vacuum, that's all I'm saying.

RACHEL

What did we even talk about last night?

GREG has steadily made his way to RACHEL's side of the bed.

GREG

I dunno. Poetry? Philosophy? The cure for world hunger?

GREG looks up, aligned for a direct eyeline to RACHEL's chest.

GREG

I didn't go on about your boobs, did I?

RACHEL

Because, how you managed to talk me into … *(Clasps SHEET to chest)* What did you say about my boobs?

GREG

I said they were great.

RACHEL

What, so the rest of me doesn't matter?

GREG

The rest of you was great too. As well as your boobs. Only I've got to know them … know *you* now. And found out there's *way* more to you. To *know about*. Not meaning your … *(Motions breasts)*. Or that you're … *(Motions overweight)*. Where'd you say those keys were?

GREG hastily crawls away.

RACHEL

Why were you at the pub anyway?

GREG

Does there ever really need to be a reason?

RACHEL

Weren't you with a buck's night? *(Recollection)* That's how we got talking.

GREG

(Evasive) Possibly. You were all stroppy about a wedding or something.

RACHEL

That was the reason I was drinking.

GREG sits up, warily scanning round for an angry fiancée.

GREG

You're getting married?

RACHEL

No. Did you listen to anything I said last night?

GREG

Sure. You were down in the dumps about your job, or your shoes or something.

RACHEL

I was getting drunk after yet another phone call from my parents about the lack of any remotely eligible men in my life whatsoever.

GREG

Ahem!

GREG strikes manly pose. RACHEL stares at him.

RACHEL

Whatsoever. How I'm too picky, followed by the usual hints I should be married by my age.

GREG

That's pretty rough. You couldn't be any older than what, 36?

RACHEL

No. I couldn't be.

GREG

It's so hard to tell in the morning light. I mean,

no one ever looks their best at … Keys. Keys.

GREG searches away from RACHEL's glare.

RACHEL notices BRA draped over BEDSIDE LAMP. Wrapped in SHEET, she tries to put BRA on.

GREG begins watching. RACHEL pulls a "Do you mind?" face. GREG shrugs and keeps watching.

Beneath SHEET, RACHEL performs a series of strange movements. (Pre-wearing an identical bra so only required to raise straps)

RACHEL drops SHEET, BRA in place.

GREG

That was quicker than I took it off.

RACHEL

About the only thing you weren't quick with, from what I vaguely remember.

GREG

Time flies in the throes of rapture.

RACHEL

I wish you'd fly off somewhere rapturous.

RACHEL grabs PYJAMA TOP from floor, dresses.

RACHEL

I was also drowning sorrows over a friend

choosing last night to announce her engagement.

GREG

Good for her!

RACHEL

To a guy that I totally fancied.

GREG

Ooh, bad for you.

RACHEL

Apparently, he's *wonderful*. Perfect, even. Her dream man. Trouble is, also my dream man.

GREG

Ouch. How did they meet?

RACHEL

I introduced them.

GREG

Hopefully not while out on a date with him.

GREG's chuckle fades at RACHEL's lack of answer.

GREG

Ooh. *Bad* for you.

RACHEL

It wasn't a date. Well, not in retrospect.

GREG

If I were you, I'd have got hammered.

RACHEL

I did get hammered. And look where that got me.

GREG

(Sultry purr, raised eyebrow) Hammered.

RACHEL is too dismayed to react.

RACHEL

She asked me to be a bridesmaid. I am *so* sick of
being a bridesmaid.

GREG

I thought girls loved it. Free booze!

RACHEL

A day squeezed in some sickly-coloured dress,
caked in make-up, fending off randy uncles soon
loses its novelty.

GREG

Never know, could be your turn next.

RACHEL

As everyone says when you *still* haven't found
someone since the last wedding they said it.

GREG

Still ... free booze.

RACHEL snatches her nearby PYJAMA BOTTOMS to don under SHEET as she speaks. (Again, pre-worn for simplicity and speed)

RACHEL

I'm tired of smiling and congratulating others enjoying the luck I want, trapped in a torture gown. Then having to explain to all—including myself—why that luck never happens to me.

GREG

You got lucky last night.

RACHEL emerges from SHEET, dressed.

RACHEL

Sure. A drunken one-off hook-up is just the way to find someone.

GREG

Doesn't have to be a one off.

RACHEL stares.

GREG

Keys?

RACHEL

Keys.

GREG

Not to your heart?

18

RACHEL shakes her head.

GREG

Actually, could you give me a reference? My
mates will never believe me, and given you've told
practically everyone already...

RACHEL shakes her head. GREG nods and resumes searching.

RACHEL's gaze lingers, reconsidering. No, don't be silly.

RACHEL wearily sits on BED, lost in thought.

RACHEL

You look and you look ...

GREG

I'm looking, I'm looking! Be patient.

RACHEL

I've been patient. They're either not interested,
not interesting, or stolen by the friend you just
introduced. I'm *over* looking and being
overlooked.

GREG

I didn't overlook you.

RACHEL

You even overlooked my name.

GREG

Who needs names when we wuz crack-a-lackin'!

RACHEL isn't receptive to his charms.

GREG sits next to RACHEL, wraps a comforting arm. Surprised, RACHEL is somewhat touched by the gesture.

GREG

Well, you have my commiserations.

RACHEL

Thank you.

GREG

And quite possibly a significant amount of my bodily fluids.

RACHEL

Thanks. That makes up for all the years of disappointment.

GREG

Does it? Goodo!

Satisfied all's fixed, GREG stands to survey the room for his keys.

GREG

Anyway, nice girl like you. Some guy is sure to swoop down and scoop you up one day.

RACHEL

(Recalls) That's what you said last night.

GREG

Really? Wow, that line hardly ever works. *(Gives an air-five)* Damn, you dawg, Greg.

RACHEL

Believe me, it wasn't your way with words that convinced me to bring you home. Mister I'm-The-Only-One-Who-Can't-Find-The-Right-Girl.

GREG fears what was revealed last night. RACHEL approaches.

RACHEL

(Baby-voice) All sad because your mates left poor widdle you on your poor widdle lonesome. *(Rubs eyes)* Boo-hoo. Boo-hoo-hoo.

GREG

You don't mean last night was ...

RACHEL

Oh yeah. Pity sex.

GREG

But pity sex doesn't count! You won't tell anyone?

RACHEL

I will not be telling *a soul* about this.

SOUND FX: RACHEL'S MOBILE SMS BEEP.

GREG

I'm not sure there's many you haven't told.

RACHEL stalks her MOBILE where she left it on BED.

RACHEL

Will you please find those keys!

RACHEL's face falls as latest SMS triggers a dismaying recollection.

RACHEL

Oh. Shit.

GREG

Didn't get your footy tips in?

RACHEL is dismayed even further.

RACHEL

Shit! *(Keeps to one problem at a time)* Do you remember what else we talked about last night?

GREG

(Sultry) Did a lot of it involve shouting my name?

RACHEL

I didn't even know your name.

GREG

Oh. Maybe that was me, then.

RACHEL

I think we posted something really very stupid.

GREG

Not one of those selfies that shows up our nostrils.

RACHEL

Worse. Look at this.

RACHEL hands MOBILE to GREG.

GREG

(Reads) "What do you mean married?"

RACHEL rubs her head with a groan, memories returning fast.

GREG

Followed by a serious string of question marks. *(Swishes)* A *serious* string. Has this person no regard for grammar?

RACHEL

After the exclamation marks.

GREG

(Swishes) "You can't get hitched in a pub, you silly cow!" That's harsh. I'd hardly call you silly.

GREG continues swishing MOBILE, nosing about.

RACHEL

Do you remember our "idea" last night?

GREG

Shagging?

RACHEL

Before the shagging.

GREG

Tequila slammers!

RACHEL

That's what led to the shagging. One of us
suggested the solution to both our problems was
a quickie wedding.

GREG

Nah.

RACHEL

While we were still drunk.

GREG

Nah.

RACHEL

Preferably by Elvis.

GREG

(Instantly recalls) Oh yeah. Why did we decide that?

RACHEL

Because he's the king of rock and roll.

GREG

No, the quickie wedding.

RACHEL

Because it would get my parents off my back and stop you crying in your beer about reaching the age where people assume you're gay.

GREG

That's actually not a bad idea.

RACHEL

Turning gay? I don't think they'd have you.

GREG

No, the quickie wedding. *(Purring)* And I think I proved my straight credentials with you last night. My *bona fides*, if you will.

RACHEL

Circumstantial evidence.

GREG

Reckon I could make it stand up in court. What's known as a *pro bono* in legal terms. And I was *not* crying into my beer! *(Looks at MOBILE)* Nice bikini selfie.

Realising he's snooping, RACHEL snatches MOBILE.

RACHEL

What it means is I have a lot of explaining to a
lot of people about something I'd really have
preferred not mentioned at all.

GREG

Bit late now.

RACHEL

It certainly is.

RACHEL gathers CLOTHES to throw onto a pile.

GREG stops her rush by softly clutching her arms.

GREG

But look on the bright side. You got laid last
night! And you know what? So did I! What a
great day to be alive!

RACHEL

Maybe I'm more choosy about the parts of my
private life I expose.

GREG

I liked the parts you exposed last night.

RACHEL shrugs his hands away to continue gathering CLOTHES.

GREG

So, you got drunk and messaged something silly.
Admittedly, to *everyone* you know. Heaven forbid!

You slept with some sexy strange man you suggested marriage to. Big deal. Who doesn't?

RACHEL

Well, it would be nice to live in your less judgemental world.

GREG sighs then pats his pockets.

GREG

Better check the damage.

GREG produces items—CREDIT CARD then BAR MAT.

GREG

Credit card—phew! Bar mat. *(Flips BAR MAT, reads)* Your phone number, I presume?

GREG holds BAR MAT for RACHEL to read.

RACHEL

(Frowns) No.

GREG quickly pockets BAR MAT as RACHEL glares in disbelief.

GREG

Oops. *(Pistol fingers)* Damn. You dawg, Greg.

GREG produces crumpled CERTIFICATE, squints to read.

GREG

What's this. *(Reading)* I, Registrar of Births,

Deaths, and Marriages for the State of … Hereby
certify the Legal Union of …

GREG and RACHEL look at each other.

GREG

I think we stole someone's Marriage Certificate.

RACHEL

Whose names are on it?

GREG

Fuck! It's mine. And someone called Rachel May
McKenzie. Probably a girl.

RACHEL

I'm Rachel May McKenzie.

GREG

You're kidding. Your middle name is *May*? It's a
month of the year.

RACHEL grabs CERTIFICATE, scans the details.

RACHEL

That's my signature. *(Shakes head)* It's a fake. Has
to be.

GREG

Looks pretty official. It has a watermark.

RACHEL

That's a beer stain.

GREG

Signed by the Registrar.

RACHEL

Someone has signed as the Registrar.

GREG

Still signed, though.

SOUND FX: RACHEL'S MOBILE SMS BEEP.

They look to MOBILE. RACHEL sits on BED, covers face.

GREG

No way. That only happens in bad Hollywood movies or dodgy reality shows.

RACHEL slowly shakes her head, more recollection arriving.

GREG

It's not that easy. We have rules here. Regulations. Quarantine. You need a celebrant or someone for a start. And they vet you. Across weeks. And you can't stay drunk that long. I've tried.

RACHEL

Do you remember Bob?

GREG

Was he that drunk old guy who staggered into our table?

RACHEL

Into and *onto*. We told him about our idea.

GREG

Ooh, over-sharing.

RACHEL

Not the shagging. About the quickie wedding.

GREG

(Recalls) Didn't we sing a song together?

RACHEL

A bit, yes. That's when Bob said he could help us.

GREG

I can hold a tune, already.

RACHEL

Do you remember what Bob did for a living?

GREG

Some boring desk job he hated? Government.
Signing stuff.

RACHEL

Yeah, *signing* stuff. *(Holds up CERTIFICATE)*
Good stuff. Like Births. Bad stuff. Like Deaths.
"And luckily for you two …"

RACHEL pushes CERTIFICATE into GREG's hands.

GREG

What was the State Registrar doing in a pub?

RACHEL

Getting legless and abusing his authority?

GREG looks at CERTIFICATE.

GREG

Nah! He couldn't have been. I mean ... *Bob.*

BOB suddenly sits up from beneath DOONA.

BOB

Now what?

RACHEL grabs SOFT TOY as a weapon, GREG assumes karate pose. BOB blinks in confusion.

BOB

Who are you?

RACHEL

What the hell are you doing here?

BOB climbs to feet to stand with authority.

BOB

I asked first. And you can start by explaining who you are before I boot you out of my bedroom!

31

RACHEL

This is my house! You're sleeping on *my* floor.

BOB looks about then rubs head wearily.

BOB

Blimey. Last night must've been a right bender.

RACHEL

It was. *(Frowns)* How often do you wake up passed out on the floor?

BOB

(Shrugs) Every now and then.

RACHEL looks to GREG in disbelief.

GREG

(Shrugs) Once or twice.

Troubled, GREG leads RACHEL aside by the arm. She shrugs his grasp indignantly.

GREG

You don't think he was here while we were ...
And might've *heard* while we were ...

RACHEL

I hope not.

GREG

Me too. I don't normally have spectators.

RACHEL

(Sharply to BOB) Did you?

BOB

Did what?

RACHEL

Hear things. Noises. Voices.

BOB

(Looks about in concern) Hearing voices?

GREG

Groaning things like "Greg! You're the best I've ever had!"

RACHEL

You'll be groaning in a minute.

BOB

I don't think so. I'm a very heavy sleeper.

RACHEL

Good.

BOB

Though I do vaguely recall someone yelling "Ride 'em cowboy".

GREG grins, points pistol finger at RACHEL.

RACHEL grabs GREG's finger in a menacing grip.

RACHEL

Have you found those keys yet?

RACHEL releases GREG's finger. He flexes circulation into his finger then continues searching.

BOB

Look, who are you? You and your boyfriend.

RACHEL

He's not my boyfriend.

GREG

And she's not mine.

BOB

(Confused) Boyfriend?

GREG

No, my girlfriend.

BOB

So, she is?

RACHEL

No, I'm not.

GREG

And I'm not hers.

BOB

Girlfriend?

GREG

I'm a guy.

BOB

I'm confused.

BOB sits on BED, shaking head.

BOB

Honestly, I don't remember anything.

RACHEL storms up to BOB.

RACHEL

You should, Bob. Because we are the people you joined together in unholy matrimony while completely stewed to your eyeballs.

GREG shows CERTIFICATE as proof. BOB takes it and groans.

BOB

Oh no. Not again.

RACHEL

You've done this before?

BOB

I really need to leave the paperwork at the office. *(Realises)* Has anyone seen a briefcase?

RACHEL

You carry marriage certificates around with you?

BOB

When I get a bit behind at work. To catch up on the backlog.

RACHEL

In a pub?

BOB

You get lonely working alone late in the office. And sometimes you just start chatting to people. Have a laugh. Sing some songs.

RACHEL

Then legally marry them.

BOB

Admittedly, this is the first time I've stuck around for the actual honeymoon.

GREG

You really take the celebrant thing to a whole new level, don't you?

RACHEL

Just as well you did hang around, because now you can un-marry us.

BOB

What, divorce?

RACHEL

Divorce. Annul. Make un-done. Whatever. Right now, so we can pretend it never happened.

BOB frowns at CERTIFICATE, holding his aching head.

GREG

But I thought we'd agreed a quickie wedding would …

RACHEL

Alcohol makes all decisions null and void. Last night was a series of bad choices on both our parts. Particularly mine.

Rejected, GREG picks up SHOES, starts untying laces.

RACHEL softens, approaches.

RACHEL

Look, I'm sure you're … *probably* a really nice guy. On your day. But last night was solely an irresponsible moment, soon to be no more.

BOB

But this is a legally binding document.

RACHEL turns, approaches BOB threateningly.

RACHEL

It's stained with beer. Surely that makes it invalid.

BOB

We usually just pretend it's a watermark.

GREG

Told you so.

RACHEL

Tear it up. This never happened.

BOB

But this is your copy. We probably posted the original on the way home. I have envelopes in my briefcase. Has anyone seen my briefcase?

GREG

I can't even find my keys.

RACHEL

The nearest post box would've been miles away!

BOB

Downhill?

RACHEL

Yes.

BOB

Thought I remembered shopping trolleys. That's probably why I woke up with these.

BOB lifts DOONA revealing TRAFFIC CONE and GNOMES. GREG is smitten by the stash.

GREG

Oh. My. God. Score!

GREG and BOB uncover more stolen treasures from beneath BED.

RACHEL

Where did we post it to?

GREG and BOB are too consumed with their booty.

RACHEL grabs TRAFFIC CONE and shouts through it into BOB's ear, startling him.

RACHEL

(Shouting through CONE) Where did we post it to?

BOB

Oh, to my Registrar's Department for filing.

RACHEL

Simple then. First thing Monday, you'll go to your Registry, bright and early, to stop it being filed.

BOB

But I'm heading away on holiday.

GREG

Oh, where are you off to?

BOB

Lovely little place down the coast. Wonderful fishing.

RACHEL

You are not going anywhere besides your office to fix this mess.

BOB

My memory's hazy, but I recall a very firm insistence of "Striking while the iron was hot".

RACHEL

I don't know how he convinced you to go through with this …

BOB

Him? You were the one who was insisting.

RACHEL is horrified. GREG winks and shoots pistol fingers.

With a groan, RACHEL sits on BED with face in hands.

RACHEL

I am never drinking again.

BOB

It's alright. Once I'm back from holiday, I'll set off the due processes. It's usually all sorted within a few weeks.

RACHEL

How many times have you done this before?

BOB

A few. Seven. Eight. Normally it doesn't matter.

RACHEL confronts BOB.

RACHEL

So, you, the State Registrar, are corrupt.

BOB

Not at all! Just a little soft-hearted.

RACHEL

Soft-headed!

BOB

The stories people tell me. So sad. And after I've had a few—quite a few—I sometimes sort of ... help things along a little.

GREG

Aww. That's quite sweet.

BOB

And you two were so excited. It seemed a shame your love be hampered by a load of bureaucracy.

RACHEL

We'd only just met.

BOB wraps arm around GREG.

BOB

I distinctly remember this one saying I was his best mate. And awfully complimentary of you.

RACHEL

Was he?

GREG

Was I?

BOB

Very much so. Particularly her boobs.

GREG

(Resumes search) Anyone seen those keys?

BOB

So, pardon me for trying to do the right thing!

RACHEL

We weren't a couple.

BOB

How was I to know?

RACHEL

It's your job to know! We only learnt our names this morning.

GREG offers hand for BOB to shake.

GREG

Greg, by the way. Real name. Liked the look of her, so I didn't slip her a false one.

BOB

And you would be … *(Checks CERTIFICATE)* Rachel May MacKenzie.

GREG

That's the little missus.

BOB

You were named after a month?

RACHEL

Surely, we needed legal witnesses.

BOB

(Reads) All of the West Morley darts club. And some bloke called Dave.

RACHEL flops to BED in defeat.

BOB

Look, I'm feeling awfully seedy. Can I have a glass of water?

RACHEL

Down the hall, through the living room. And don't wake my housemate!

BOB lays CERTIFICATE next to RACHEL then carefully opens DOOR, checking his way before departing OUT.

GREG hums Wedding March, sashaying to BED, sits next to her.

RACHEL

I can't think of a worse way to wake up to a weekend.

GREG

Oh, I don't know. As far as mistaken marriages go, in terms of looks, personality, sex factor …

RACHEL looks to him in surprise, complimented.

GREG

You could've done a whole lot worse.

RACHEL

Thank you.

GREG

How do you know I'm not a Prince Charming?

RACHEL

I have my suspicions.

GREG takes CERTIFICATE. A thought strikes.

GREG

Though this does work out like we planned. I've clocked up some legitimacy, and you're one step back from becoming a mad old cat lady.

RACHEL gives withering look.

GREG

They don't have to be real cats.

RACHEL

What do you mean, legitimacy?

GREG

(Holds CERTIFICATE) This here is proof of investment in a serious relationship.

RACHEL

For what, twelve hours?

GREG

No one can call me a commitment-phobe now.

GREG carefully folds CERTIFICATE, puts it in pocket, pats it.

GREG

Thanks to this baby, I'm a certified commodity. Social proof. Market value. Not some lonesome flaky guy no one wants. Someone *married* me.

RACHEL

For an evening.

GREG

Someone wanted to spend the rest of *their* life with *me*.

RACHEL

We probably only wanted to split the taxi fare.

GREG

Someone wanted to hold and to *have* me.

RACHEL

It's getting annulled.

GREG stops, concerned.

GREG

You mean divorced.

RACHEL

Annulled. As though it never happened.

GREG

But it did. From now on, I can legitimately *choose* to be single. With all the mature experience and sexual mystery of the young divorcee ...

RACHEL

Annullee.

GREG

They'll try to work out the enigma. "Did she leave him?" "Did he leave her?"

RACHEL

I left you, definitely.

GREG

See, even you're drawn in by the mystery. It's scientifically proven. Girls ignore single guys, but ... *(Holds up ring finger)* ... put a ring on it. Voom! Interest galore.

RACHEL holds her unadorned hand for him to see.

RACHEL

What ring?

GREG checks carefully, sniffs, then picks a crumb and tastes it.

GREG

Cheezel crumbs. *(Aghast)* You ate my symbol of eternal love.

GREG gives own ring finger a sniff.

GREG

Onion ring. My favourite. You shouldn't have.

RACHEL

I didn't.

GREG

Anyway, I'll buy myself a cheapy ring somewhere, then let the divorcee string of flings begin. *(Pats pocket)* I got me a ticket to ride.

RACHEL

And exactly how long is this string of flings?

GREG

Philosophy. I like that in a girl. How long is a piece of string? How many roads must a man walk down?

RACHEL

I wish you'd bugger off down a road. Men using the commitment-phobe excuse are usually playboys or whiny single guys. Which are you?

GREG

(*Defensive*) I've had relationships.

RACHEL

Long-term ones?

GREG sits on BED and dons SHOES.

GREG

Depends how you define long-term.

RACHEL

Years? Months? *Weekends?*

GREG feels obliged to admit.

GREG

Three weeks is my record. Rounding up. She was away the middle weekend.

RACHEL

To be honest, I admire her effort to last that long with you.

GREG ties SHOE laces in silence.

Realising she's hit a nerve, RACHEL sits on BED.

RACHEL

I'm surprised to hear that. I'm sorry it hasn't worked out for you.

GREG nods a wounded thanks.

RACHEL

"Don't worry, nice guy like you, I'm sure some girl will swoop down and scoop you up one day".

GREG

Maybe I'm just picky.

RACHEL

Yeah. Picky. That would be it.

RACHEL lies on her front, chin on hands.

RACHEL

That's what they tell me too. Like I have to choose because no one chooses me. *(Sighs)* Maybe in life's box of chocolates, we're the Turkish Delights no one ever selects.

GREG

Actually, I quite like Turkish Delight.

RACHEL

(Zero enthusiasm) Hooray, I'm saved.

GREG

You don't particularly come across as a "soft centre". More a … hard toffee that might take a tooth for the unwary. Approach with caution.

RACHEL

I'm approachable. Aren't I? You approached.

GREG

Didn't we more happen upon each other.
(Corrects) Onto each other. *(Corrects) Into* each
other. I think we just met.

RACHEL sits up, disappointed.

RACHEL

I am approachable. Mostly. I *am* a soft centre. A
Peppermint Crème. Sharp and refreshing.

GREG

More like a Coconut Rough.

RACHEL

A *Bounty* – hidden but worth discovering.

GREG

You were a Rum Old Truffle when we met.

RACHEL

A *Chocolat Ganache*. Lush, rich and velvety.

Sensing a game is afoot, GREG moves closer on BED.

GREG

And you've ganache-ed teeth at me ever since.

RACHEL

A *Caramel Rapture* then.

GREG

Rupture?

RACHEL

Rapture.

GREG appraises this, lying on his front on BED by RACHEL.

GREG

Or perhaps ... a *Mon Cherie Surprise.*

RACHEL

You surprise me.

GREG

I'm full of them.

RACHEL

You're full of something.

GREG

Maybe I was inspired.

RACHEL

Maybe I'm impressed.

GREG

Maybe a soft centre after all.

RACHEL

Maybe. If someone took a bite to find out.

A moment of lingering eye contact.

RACHEL

Even a nibble might crack the surface.

They slowly lean in towards each other, when ...

SOUND FX: RACHEL'S MOBILE SMS BEEP.

RACHEL's head flops to the BED, the moment lost.

DOOR opens, BOB pops his head round.

BOB

I think that was your telephone.

RACHEL

What do you want now?

BOB

Would it be totally out of the question if I were
to have a bath?

RACHEL

Yes, totally.

BOB

No bathtub?

RACHEL strides over to confront BOB. GREG sits up.

RACHEL

Go home. Have one there.

BOB

If you only knew the shouting and screaming that would involve.

GREG

Your hot water a bit unpredictable too?

BOB

There'll be plenty of hot water. From the wife, after another night out.

RACHEL

Passing out in a bedroom of a girl half your age.

BOB

(Frowns) I'm not in my seventies.

RACHEL looks to GREG for support, but he's looking away.

BOB

Anyway, I only want a quick one. In and out. You'd barely notice.

RACHEL and GREG look to him, unsure what they heard.

BOB

A wash. Barely a rinse.

RACHEL

No, you'll wake my housemate. And the last thing she needs to see is a naked old man. Not even the last thing—it's not a thing she needs, ever.

BOB

You just feel a bit crusty after a rough old sleep in your work clothes.

RACHEL

Go home then!

BOB

Without a wash?

RACHEL

Yes!

BOB

But I'm making toast.

RACHEL

Who said you could make toast?

BOB

You want some?

GREG raises his hand eagerly.

RACHEL

You're going too.

GREG

On an empty stomach?

RACHEL

This is not a bed and breakfast!

BOB

Certainly isn't. Most of those have a bathtub.

BOB departs, closing DOOR.

GREG

How's he going to eat toast in the shower?

RACHEL

He's not. He's going, and so are you.

GREG

I thought we were nibbling your soft bits.

RACHEL

The box is *closed.*

The moment definitely passed, GREG resumes looking for his keys.

GREG

What's the hurry? In a few weeks' time, Bob divorces us …

RACHEL

Annuls us.

GREG

Then we go our separate divorcee ways with the version of the story we prefer. You tell it your way, I cash in on mine. At the very least, it's a tale for the grandkids.

GREG and RACHEL look to each other in concern.

RACHEL

Did you use …?

GREG

I sort of assumed you …?

GREG and RACHEL look around for discarded contraceptives.

They at each other, concerned.

GREG

I'm sure we'll be *perfectly* fine.

Unimpressed, RACHEL resumes tidying her room.

RACHEL

You might feel validated boasting of a sham marriage in your name. I don't. It's hard enough finding someone without baggage like that.

GREG

I'll change your name to protect your innocence.

RACHEL

Do you even remember it now?

GREG shies from answering.

RACHEL

There will be no stories told of this, changed
names or not. Believe me, word gets around.

GREG

You can embellish your version however you
want. Add some mystery and allure. Everyone
exaggerates on the chat-up anyway.

RACHEL

Are you saying you lied to get me into bed?

GREG moves to a defensive position behind CHAIR.

GREG

… which bits?

RACHEL

I don't remember. Which *bits*? Did you say
anything truthful to me last night?

GREG

I dunno, I don't remember either.

RACHEL takes out frustrations on fluffing PILLOWS.

RACHEL

I'm not using this debacle as some gimmick to get my leg over.

GREG

It would keep your parents off your back.

RACHEL

I'm sure they'd be pleased with my drunken marriage to a stranger. It's every parent's dream.

GREG

They'll be delighted! I can even pop in to meet them if it helps.

RACHEL roughly fluffs PILLOW with a stern glare.

GREG

Or perhaps not.

RACHEL sits on BED clutching PILLOW in a hug.

GREG

Come on, we're married! You're not the bridesmaid. It'll take a few weeks anyway, let's have fun with it.

RACHEL

It's not taking weeks. Bob is sorting it Monday.

GREG sidles amorously towards the BED.

GREG

Maybe. *(Seductive)* Still gives us the weekend for
the honeymoon.

RACHEL

We are *not* married.

GREG

One soggy certificate says otherwise.

GREG slinks on all fours across BED, purring up to RACHEL.

GREG

Seems a shame to waste the opportunity.

RACHEL turns, meeting GREG eye to eye.

RACHEL

If you wish to remain the biological male in our
coupling, you'll think your next move *very carefully.*

A beat, then GREG warily backtracks off BED, onto CHAIR.

GREG

We're still married though. Think of it as a road-
test. See how it corners, fiddle with the controls.
(Suggestive) Take her out for a spin.

RACHEL

You know what you can take a spin on?

RACHEL throws PILLOW into place, resumes making BED.

GREG

And what a break from solo stress! Single people
die younger, you know. Wearing themselves out,
putting on a show for any off-chance they meet.
But get hitched, you can relax. Let it all go a bit.

GREG sags his belly, pats his gut.

RACHEL

That's quite the prize for any future wife.

GREG

She can pop on a few pounds if she likes. All the
more lovin' to grab hold of.

GREG gives RACHEL a wink.

RACHEL

Great! Slipping standards—there's something to
look forward to.

GREG

Slipping into something more comfortable.

RACHEL

I'm not settling into some survival of the fattest,
whose only shared interest is a television remote.
There must be better than apathetic convenience.

GREG

If you can find it. If not, given time, "near
enough" could become something great.

RACHEL

No offence, Greg, but I've kissed enough frogs
to know they just stay frogs. Or turn into toads.

GREG shrugs off the insult. RACHEL continues tidying.

GREG

Of course, in some countries, this sort of thing
happens all the time.

RACHEL

Drunken regrettable bonking?

GREG

Arranged marriages where the newlyweds don't
meet till their wedding. Those work out fine.

RACHEL

They have family members to filter out losers.
Here, sadly, we only have sobriety.

GREG

I wouldn't mind a family arranging their daughter
to marry me.

RACHEL

The Addams Family maybe?

GREG

But it can work. Two strangers pushed together
with no choice but to make a go of it. Making
something wonderful from nothing. Whereas
here we hook up with all our expectations, then

get disappointed when they're not met. Maybe we've got it the wrong way round.

RACHEL

Are you saying I didn't meet expectations?

GREG

We were too drunk for expectations!

RACHEL flings PILLOW, GREG ducks.

GREG

Are we so far from that, with our *unarranged* marriage? Who's to say we couldn't make something wonderful from nothing too?

RACHEL

Common sense and practically everyone.

RACHEL sits on end of BED.

GREG

But it is nice though, when it does work.

GREG draws near, sliding onto BED.

GREG

Till death do us part. In sickness and in health.

GREG slides closer to RACHEL.

GREG

Two as one, sharing all that life throws our way.

GREG leans in slowly.

GREG

Love over time. Real love, not just shagging. Nurtured. Evolving. The real thing.

RACHEL

You are not sleeping with me again so don't even try the sensitive stuff.

GREG immediately stands.

GREG

Right, let's get this dude annulled then.

FEMALE SCREAM from OFF stage.

GREG

Wow. Bob really took that to heart.

JANE bursts in, wearing pyjamas and ugg boots.

JANE

(Points out DOOR) Who is that? *(Points to GREG)* Who is that?

RACHEL

(Weary) Jane, this is Greg, a guy I met at the pub, then brought home after accidentally marrying.

GREG inconspicuously smoothes hair, clothes, and checks breath.

RACHEL

In the kitchen is the State Registrar of Births, Deaths and Marriages who performed the ceremony, and I'll be suing in the near future.

JANE

That's a relief. For a minute out there, I thought you'd really let your standards slip.

RACHEL appraises GREG.

RACHEL

Oh, they've slipped, all right.

Too smitten to notice sarcasm, GREG turns on the charm.

GREG

You must be the housemate?

JANE

That's right. I'm Jane.

GREG

Lovely to meet you, Jane. Sorry, I'm not normally such a mess first thing in the morning.

JANE

That's okay, I'm not normally so loud-and-bursting-into-other-people's-bedrooms.

GREG

Cool.

JANE

Like, "Hey, just Jane bursting in randomly again!"
Just something she does.

GREG

(Nods, tongue-tied) Yeah ... Cool.

JANE

Bursting in like a mad person. "Heeeere's Janey!"

JANE does "Psycho" knife movements and violin noises.

GREG

(Less sure) Yeah. ... Cool.

JANE

Who knows what I might come across.

RACHEL

A restraining order?

JANE

Exactly.

GREG

Cool.

JANE

Yeah, cool.

RACHEL regards them, smiling at each other.

RACHEL

Aaanyway, now introductions are over …

JANE

So, dodgy-old-kitchen-guy—who is he?

GREG

That's Bob. He married us. *(Realises)* Not that it's legally binding, of course. I am actually single.

RACHEL

Not technically.

GREG

But morally, certainly.

RACHEL

Legally *not*.

JANE

Single but married?

GREG

Sort of, sort of not.

RACHEL

Sort of yes-we-bloody-are!

GREG shrugs and discreetly shakes head to JANE.

RACHEL

It turns out our friend Bob out there *officially* joins people in matrimony despite all concerned being pissed out of their minds.

JANE

Wasn't that the plot of a Sex in the City episode?

GREG

I don't remember that one.

RACHEL and JANE look to him.

GREG

It's often on in the waiting room at the dentist when I—ooh, look at that!

GREG is instantly consumed with interest in a GNOME.

JANE

This episode was exactly like you guys. Only in a zoo. And everyone had beards. *(Thinks)* Maybe that was a dream. Anyway, a couple on the radio the other day rang in about their drunk marriage, so it's hardly a big deal. Wow, cool gnome!

JANE joins GREG who proudly displays the various stolen items.

GREG

That's not all we got, look at these.

RACHEL

What did they do about it?

JANE is too distracted with GREG's goodies.

RACHEL

Jane! Focus. What did they do?

JANE

Who?

RACHEL

The couple on the radio. Did they cancel their marriage?

JANE

I think they just wanted attention. The usual types using a crazy marriage to make themselves more interesting. I mean, how desperate.

GREG

(Scoffs in agreement) Desperados.

JANE

You should ring in with your story. You might win a shopping voucher.

RACHEL

Well, Greg, you might get your wish after all.

GREG

(Not listening whatsoever) Mm, yeah. So, Jane, what do you do? Model work? Actress? Dancer?

JANE

Hardly. I'm a just a linguistic anthropologist.

GREG

... Oh.

JANE

Though I guess I do a bit of statistical modelling.

GREG

I knew it! From very first sight, I just knew you had to be a model.

RACHEL

Excuse me. If you're finished chatting up my housemate ...

JANE

He wasn't chatting me up.

GREG

I was a bit.

JANE

(Giggles) Really?

RACHEL drags GREG up and aside by his arm.

RACHEL

May I remind you, you're my legal husband.

GREG

You want it annulled.

RACHEL

That is not the point. Well, it is *a* point, but a crap one. How do you think I feel?

GREG

Don't worry, you can see other people, too.

RACHEL

Yes, but you're seeing them in my bedroom. Given what I said earlier about friends stealing my love interests...

GREG reacts to his classification as a love interest.

RACHEL

... don't you think it's ever so *completely* insensitive to cop off with my housemate in front of me?

GREG

You've been telling me to go away all morning.

RACHEL

Yes. But maybe given time to gather myself, weigh things up, eventually finding some non-committal reason to call, like some item deliberately left behind—you know, the traditional protocol—then maybe I'd reconsider.

GREG

I was going to leave something behind: Myself.

RACHEL

I mean a considered romantic follow-up, not

blatant opportunism.

GREG
No, you've lost me.

RACHEL
No. You've lost me.

BOB wanders in with FRYPAN.

BOB
Righto. Found the bacon so who's for a fry up?

GREG and JANE raise hands with a cheer.

RACHEL
Jane, you don't even know him.

BOB strides over and shakes JANE's hand.

BOB
The name's Bob. How do you like your breakfast?

RACHEL bursts forward to break the bonhomie.

RACHEL
Enough! You, Bob—down to your office right
now to do whatever it takes to stop that
certificate reaching wherever it's going.

GREG
But he's making us bacon.

BOB gives GREG a sly elbow to the ribs.

BOB

I think maybe you two made enough of that last
night, eh?

*RACHEL glares, BOB's chortling dies out. GREG acts innocent for
JANE's behalf.*

BOB

There's really nothing I can do. With my
signature and stamp it'll go straight into the
system. I have a very efficient department.
Especially when I'm not there.

RACHEL

You're responsible, you fix it.

BOB

But that'll need explanations. The Attorney
General might be called in. With my track history,
I could get the sack.

RACHEL

Is that such a bad thing?

BOB

Why should I lose my job for being soft-hearted
to those *demanding* the marriage in the first place?

GREG

We were *pretty* drunk, though. *(Realises, cover to
JANE)* The only reason why I went along with it.

RACHEL

You bastard!

GREG

(To JANE) Just a bit of a joke, really.

RACHEL

From what I remember, it largely was.

GREG

"Ride 'em, cowboy."

RACHEL turns to BOB. GREG innocently shrugs to JANE.

RACHEL

Surely you can annul it!

BOB

Not if the marriage was consummated.

GREG

(Worried) Only a bit.

RACHEL

Barely a bit.

BOB

Sadly, getting "a bit" makes annulment out of the question. I'm unsure of the detailed ins and outs, but from a legal point of view, things happened.

RACHEL

So, my marital history gets ruined by a drunken

fling over barely after it started.

GREG

Believe me Jane, there were no complaints at the time. Not that I'm only interested in …

JANE

Bob's right, you know.

GREG

Is he? Sure. What about?

JANE

(Rote) A marriage can only be annulled if there was no act of consummation, one party made malicious deception, wasn't of sane frame of mind, or the celebrant's credentials were suspect.

GREG and RACHEL turn accusingly to BOB. They all then look to JANE, surprised by her erudite summation.

JANE

I read an article on ill-considered weddings. It was called "Oops, I Committed Again".

RACHEL

Off our faces on Tequila cannot count as a sane frame of mind.

BOB

You seemed fine to me.

RACHEL

You were more soused than we were! What
happens when I want to get married?

BOB

Again?

RACHEL

Properly. Courted. Wooed. Lavished with
attention. Sober. I want a clean slate, not be pre-
soiled goods.

BOB

Given last night's efforts, wearing white may be a
little presumptuous.

GREG steps in to BOB's rescue before RACHEL explodes.

GREG

How's that bacon going?

Grateful for escape, BOB departs with a wave of FRYPAN.

RACHEL sits on BED, weary.

*JANE nods to GREG to comfort RACHEL. GREG shrugs "what
do I do?", but JANE nods insistently towards RACHEL.*

GREG sits next to RACHEL, putting a hesitant arm around her.

GREG

You're not *that* pre-soiled. *(Glances back to BED)*

Quite a lot of it went over there.

JANE backs away with "eww" face, providing opportunity to step on and discover KEYS, picking them up.

RACHEL

From day one, we're taught to crave the dream marriage. Disney Princesses. Wedding-Day Barbie. Glass slippers. Hurry, though, because you also need to have kids. But don't forget your career! Then work so hard you never have time or energy to meet Mr Right. No biggy. But never fear because your mother will remind you with *every* phone call. You've got to nab your Prince Charming at any cost, without scaring them off with too many … *(Regards GREG)* Rumpelstiltskins along the way. No offence.

GREG

None taken.

RACHEL

Really?

GREG

Why? Which one was I? Oh. Okay, some then.

RACHEL

And you wonder why it matters if the story doesn't go to the plan everyone expects? Magic fairy godmothers can only wish away so much.

JANE

(Wistful) I had a Wedding-Day Barbie.

GREG *gazes adoringly at JANE.*

JANE

She came with a full-length wedding dress, a carriage with four white horses, and a signed pre-nuptial agreement. Solicitor Barbie had Ken's arse on toast if he set so much as one foot astray.

GREG's *interest wilts.*

RACHEL

And maybe I'd like my own one day of perfect.

JANE *nods, signalling GREG to do something.*

GREG

So, in a way, we guys are doing you a favour.

RACHEL *and* JANE *look at him, confused.*

GREG

There it is: your wedding day. The one day where you're the princess. The bestest, happiest day of your life. Surely, it's all downhill from then on.

RACHEL

It certainly has been today.

GREG

So, being all cagey, shying away and putting off,
we guys keep that pinnacle ahead for you to look
forward to, rather than looking back knowing
your best ever day has already been. You say it's
lack of commitment, when actually we're keeping
your glass half-full for as long as possible.

RACHEL

I'd like to drown you in a something half-full.

JANE

I can't wait to have a full white wedding.

GREG is instantly transfixed by JANE's happy vision.

JANE

All my family and friends in a big church
decorated in flowers. My dress of satin and lace.
And the *biggest* party imaginable.

GREG

You would look *fantastic*. So, your dad must be
pretty rich, then?

JANE

Oh, he's loaded. He's on the board of a brewery.

GREG's jaw drops with a little awestruck whimper.

GREG

I think there's nothing better than a big
traditional wedding.

RACHEL

As opposed to hooking up while pissed in a pub?

GREG

Shh!

Furious, RACHEL stands to loom over GREG.

RACHEL

Don't shh me! How would you like it if I cracked on to your housemate in front of you?

GREG

Quite a lot really, she's a stunner. Her boyfriend might have something to say about that, though. Actually, no, he'd be quite keen to see it too.

RACHEL sits on BED having had enough.

RACHEL

How can I lock the entire world out of my bedroom this morning?

JANE

Maybe shutting yourself away is the whole problem. Your perfect man is hardly going to walk in here and say "So, how about it".

RACHEL

Why not, everyone else seems to be today.

BOB enters wearing APRON with FRYPAN.

BOB

So. How about—

RACHEL

Out!

BOB departs.

JANE

It'll happen for you someday. Probably.
Meantime, you have the next best thing.

RACHEL

Which is?

JANE

You could be one of my bridesmaids.

RACHEL

Fan-tastic.

RACHEL sinks her head into her hands, over it all.

JANE

For the record, though, my wedding is going to
be *huge*. Dad said so.

GREG

He sounds a very sensible man. So, *owner* of the
brewery, or just on the Board?

RACHEL

Greg! Please … keys.

JANE produces KEYS she found.

JANE

Are these them?

GREG jumps up to join JANE. She exchanges KEYS.

GREG

Cool! Cheers.

They stand coyly then GREG realises this is the end of the encounter.

GREG

Oh. … Well, I guess this means I'll be going.

JANE bites her lip and nods.

GREG

Pretty soon.

JANE

Almost like … now.

GREG

(To RACHEL) Though we should swap numbers, Rachel. Just in case Bob can't … After all we've been through.

RACHEL

No.

GREG is crestfallen. RACHEL sighs.

RACHEL

But I'm sure if Jane gave you *her* number, she
could pass any messages on.

JANE

Good plan!

GREG

Cool.

JANE

Excellent.

JANE waits for GREG who freezes, unsure how to proceed.

RACHEL lays back with a groan.

RACHEL

Just ask the girl out! Don't mind me.

RACHEL covers head with PILLOW.

GREG

Good point. *(To JANE, still struggling)* Do you
need a lift anywhere?

JANE

Okay!

GREG

Great. Where?

JANE

I dunno.

GREG

Exactly the direction I was heading.

JANE

I'll get my bag.

GREG

Except, I have absolutely no idea where my car is.

JANE

I guess we just roam around until we find it.

GREG

That could be a lot of roaming.

JANE

You'd better be pretty charming then. *(Punches GREG's arm)* You can buy me a Frappuccino.

JANE eagerly departs.

GREG delightedly watches her go, then rubs the arm she punched.

GREG

Oww.

Remembering RACHEL, GREG approaches BED guiltily.

GREG

Thanks for a great night.

Head still under PILLOW, RACHEL raises hand, gives thumbs up.

GREG

I hope you don't mind, if Jane and I were to …

RACHEL's hand signals "OK", then arm flops down.

GREG continues to linger.

GREG

You never know, if she swoops, I might even let
myself be scooped.

No reaction. GREG makes to leave then stops.

GREG

Of course, if it doesn't work out with Jane …
Given that we technically still are …

RACHEL's hand points forcefully to door.

GREG

I'd better be off then.

RACHEL's hand wearily waves goodbye.

GREG waves back then moves to DOOR. He stops then approaches BED, takes RACHEL's wilting hand, plants a kiss, and departs.

RACHEL's hand hangs sadly, then drops despondently.

SOUND FX: RACHEL'S MOBILE RINGTONE.

RACHEL sits up, then winces at MOBILE caller ID, answers.

RACHEL

Oh, hi Mum. *Exactly* the person to speak to this morning. ... What? How did you hear about that? ... No Mum, I haven't got married.

RACHEL crosses fingers on free hand to exempt her from the white lie.

RACHEL

Well, I've no idea why Amy would tell you something like that. She actually lies quite a lot, Mum. And steals things. She's really not to be trusted.

BOB enters with PLATE with BACON then makes himself comfortable on the BED next to RACHEL.

RACHEL stares at BOB in disbelief while listening to MOBILE.

RACHEL

Of course I'd tell you if I got married, Mum.

BOB

Lovely bit of breakfast. Bunch up!

RACHEL

Just the tv, Mum. I'll mute it. *(Covers MOBILE)*
Excuse me.

BOB

Oh! Manners. *(Offers PLATE)* Toasty soldier?

RACHEL

I'm going to have you sued, you know.

RACHEL snatches BACON from PLATE, to BOB's dismay.

BOB

I'll sort it out on Monday.

RACHEL

All of it. Without a trace.

BOB

Like it never happened.

BOB waves a finger towards her face, eventually landing on her nose.

BOB

Bippetty. Boppetty. Boo.

RACHEL

Take your finger off my nose.

BOB

Okay.

BOB withdraws his finger. RACHEL resumes call.

RACHEL

Sorry, Mum, I ... Yes, I know. Yes, *I know.*

BOB

You know what I think?

RACHEL

(Covers MOBILE) That it's possible to be
strangled with a strip of bacon?

BOB

The legal stuff, the rigmarole ... none of it
matters. All that's important is being able to gaze
into the eyes of that special person, every
morning. Just you, just them, and the delight of
being together. Each and every day, for the rest
of your days. To know you love, and *are* loved by
that other person.

RACHEL lowers MOBILE onto her chest to listen.

BOB

I found her, you know. That one person. As
beautiful as the first time I laid eyes upon her.
And each time I lay beside this woman I hold
above all others, I think to myself as I always will
... if only she'd leave her husband, and I could
escape the wife, I'd marry her on the spot.

RACHEL deflates.

BOB

Take your time. Less *over*-looking. Don't rush in
and chain yourself to the wrong one for what will
seem like forever. That's the mistake I made.

RACHEL offers some BACON. BOB takes a piece.

BOB

At least until I learn to forge those signatures.
(Wistful) And I'm getting closer, you know. Day
by day. Day by day.

*RACHEL regards BOB as he munches BACON, then returns to
MOBILE, emboldened.*

RACHEL

Actually Mum, I'll *tell* you when I find the right
person. In fact, I'll shout it to the whole world.
Maybe not by drunken phone broadcast. But in
the meantime, it's probably a lovely morning out.
Just right for a *me*-day. Which means quite
enough of you.

*RACHEL ends the call then swaps MOBILE for the WINE
GLASS with last night's dregs on BEDSIDE TABLE.*

She taps BOB's PLATE in a toast.

RACHEL

To fresh starts.

*RACHEL swigs a medicinal gulp then grimaces—it's horrendous.
BOB munches BACON happily.*

RACHEL

So, how about *that*.

*RACHEL looks to DOOR, but no perfect person walks in on cue.
Her enthusiasm ebbs.*

She sighs.

RACHEL

Maybe tomorrow, then.

A sigh, a shrug, then RACHEL swigs again.

LIGHTS DOWN.

END OF ACT ONE

ACT TWO

Morning, a Sunday. RACHEL is under DOONA in BED, asleep in PYJAMA PANTS and a t-shirt TOP.

BRIDESMAID DRESS is draped over CLOTHES RACK. RACHEL's MOBILE sits on her DRESSER.

JANE raps on DOOR, calls from OFF.

JANE

Rachel, are you getting ready?

RACHEL raises a lazy hand with a sleepy groan.

JANE

Are you getting ready?

RACHEL

Yes.

JANE

I *will* come in and check.

RACHEL

Not if I lock my door first.

RACHEL sits up, regards DOOR so very far away.

RACHEL

(Weary) I'm not locking the door.

RACHEL collapses back onto BED.

JANE opens DOOR, edges head in. Her hair is wrapped in TOWEL, and she is wearing a BATHROBE.

JANE
Are you nearly ready?

RACHEL
Nearly.

JANE
Is that nearly nearly, or nearly not even close?

RACHEL
Right onto it.

JANE
Because we'll need to leave for the church soon.

RACHEL checks time on MOBILE on BEDSIDE TABLE.

RACHEL
Three hours is not soon. Three hours is two and a half hours before soon.

JANE
If your dress doesn't fit, we need to tell the seamstress straight away.

RACHEL
Not on a Sunday morning.

JANE

She said straight away.

RACHEL

She didn't mean on a Sunday. It's a day of rest.
For normal people anyway.

JANE

Do you want my mum to make you breakfast? Or
lunch. Or neither.

RACHEL

Toast?

JANE

Will you be up soon?

RACHEL

I'm already up … ish.

JANE

Great. *(Shouts back into house)* Mum! Rachel wants
breakfast.

JANE departs, leaving DOOR open.

JANE

Yes, I hope she'll still fit in her dress too.

*RACHEL glares then laboriously rises from BED. She takes the
distasteful apricot-coloured BRIDESMAID DRESS from
CLOTHES RACK and holds it before herself.*

RACHEL

Sweet baby Jesus.

RACHEL tosses BRIDESMAID DRESS back over RACK.

Plodding to BED, RACHEL takes PILLOW to make the bed but instead hugs PILLOW and climbs back under DOONA groaning.

A beat.

GREG sneaks in, silently closing DOOR behind him. He leans ear to DOOR to confirm no one is coming.

GREG moves to BED but hesitates on seeing RACHEL asleep. He steps forward to nudge her but decides against it. He returns to DOOR and raps quietly.

No reaction from RACHEL.

Wincing, GREG risks rapping a smidgeon louder.

RACHEL

I'm getting up!

GREG waits expectantly. No movement from RACHEL.

GREG

No, you're not.

RACHEL sits up and covers herself with PILLOW.

RACHEL

What are you doing here? What are you doing *in
here?*

GREG

Relax. I've seen you in your pyjamas before. And
out of them, for that matter.

RACHEL

Not as my housemate's fiancée. What do you
want?

GREG

I need your advice.

RACHEL

Sure: Don't ever sneak into my room again.

GREG

I knocked.

RACHEL

From the inside.

GREG

Still knocked though.

RACHEL

How long have you been in here? *(Suspicious)*
Were you hiding in my wardrobe?

GREG *glances around room.*

GREG

You have a wardrobe?

RACHEL

(Points) Over there.

GREG squints at some off-stage object, stepping closer to confirm.

GREG

Oh! So you do. You should try putting the clothes *in* it instead of *over* it.

RACHEL

Jane's in the kitchen. With her mum.

GREG

I know. I *really* don't want to see her.

RACHEL

Her mum probably feels the same about you.

GREG

Her mum's fine. In small doses. I mean, Jane. Or more importantly, that she doesn't see me.

RACHEL

You've got it the wrong way round. It's the bride who isn't meant to be seen on the wedding day. Anyway, it's only the practice run today.

GREG

Exactly. And that's the thing I need to do.

RACHEL

Practice?

GREG

No. Run.

DOOR opens and JANE backs in with a PLATE with TOAST and a COFFEE MUG.

GREG dives behind far side of BED to hide.

JANE

Here we go.

JANE sees RACHEL in bed, still clutching PILLOW.

JANE

Are you ever getting up?

RACHEL tosses PILLOW onto GREG, further concealing him, then springs from BED towards JANE.

RACHEL

Sure am!

RACHEL takes PLATE and COFFEE, blocking JANE's view.

RACHEL

Thanks! I'm famished.

JANE

Because you slept in again. Does the dress fit?

RACHEL

What dress?

JANE

The bridesmaid dress.

RACHEL

Just about to try it on.

JANE takes PLATE back.

JANE

Maybe check it fits first. Just in case.

RACHEL takes PLATE back.

RACHEL

I'm not starving myself for the next fortnight.

JANE

You haven't exactly starved yourself since the fitting. Just remember—apricot shows.

RACHEL

Then why dress your bridesmaids in apricot?

JANE

Because it's my favourite yoghurt flavour. Meh. Everyone's looking at the bride on the big day anyway.

RACHEL

And wondering why her closest friends came
dressed as fruit desserts.

JANE

You want to look your best for my Cousin Geoff.

RACHEL

Exactly why I shouldn't wear an apricot dress. ...
He is definitely coming?

JANE

I told him all about you.

RACHEL

So, he's bailed out then.

JANE

You're so pessimistic. He was *very* interested
when I described you.

RACHEL

Very?

JANE

Very.

RACHEL

And he's hunky.

JANE

Very hunky. Very single. And very very keen.

RACHEL

… I'll try the dress in a minute.

Satisfied, JANE moves to DOOR.

JANE

Hurry eating your toast. Mum needs the plate.

RACHEL

We have heaps of plates.

JANE

And there'll be heaps of people here for the
wedding breakfast. Every plate counts.

RACHEL

But today's only the practice run.

JANE

She's practicing the catering. That plate's
earmarked for Aunt Julia. And you don't want to
get between Aunt Julia and a cheesy nibble,
believe me. Everything *has* to be perfect. No
shortages. No food poisonings. *(Whispers)* Try the
dress!

JANE departs, closing DOOR.

GREG is instantly up and over to RACHEL.

GREG

Thanks! *(Notices PLATE)* Ooh, thanks!

GREG takes TOAST and eagerly takes a bite.

RACHEL

What do you mean "run"?

GREG speaks with mouthful of TOAST.

GREG

(Garbled) I think I'm getting cold feet.

RACHEL takes TOAST from him.

RACHEL

What?

GREG raises hand as he finishes chewing, then takes COFFEE from RACHEL and drinks. When eventually done …

GREG

I think I'm getting cold feet.

GREG hands COFFEE back, then takes TOAST again.

RACHEL

Is that all? Everyone does.

RACHEL nearly takes a drink of COFFEE then remembers he has already drunk from it. She sits on end of BED.

RACHEL

You're taking a big step—a big incredibly stupid step. It's hardly surprising you have a few nerves.

GREG

This is more than nerves. It's like ... sheer terror.
I think I might've rushed into things.

RACHEL

You have. Again. Mindless spontaneous weddings
are hardly new ground for you.

GREG

It's different this time.

RACHEL

You were sober when you proposed?

GREG

(Shrugs) ... More sober.

GREG sits on BED near RACHEL, glumly bites TOAST.

*RACHEL holds PLATE to catch GREG's crumbs. GREG places
TOAST on PLATE then wipes fingers on DOONA. RACHEL
glares, but GREG blithely takes COFFE for another sip.*

RACHEL

You and Jane have dated almost six months. She's
moving in with you—God help her. That's
almost conventional by your standards. It's also
conventional to get the jitters near the big day.

GREG shrugs, hands COFFEE back.

RACHEL

You do love her, don't you?

GREG picks up TOAST, averting eye contact.

GREG

Sure. Largely. To an extent.

RACHEL

"To an extent"? Why did you propose to
someone you only love "to an extent"?

GREG

I did love her. Do. Did. Until I proposed.

RACHEL

Believe me, Greg, Jane is the best you could ever
possibly get. Ever.

GREG

(Looks to RACHEL) Maybe not ever.

A knock on the DOOR.

JANE

Are you decent?

GREG flings TOAST then dives behind far side of BED.
RACHEL rushes to DOOR to block view by standing innocently with
COFFEE and PLATE.

103

RACHEL

Um, sort of.

JANE enters and is dismayed by RACHEL.

JANE

You're still in your pyjamas! *(Sees TOAST on floor)*
If you didn't like the toast, you should've said.

RACHEL

I ... sneezed.

*They look at PLATE in RACHEL's hand then at TOAST quite
some distance away.*

JANE

Wow. Geisundheit.

JANE takes PLATE.

JANE

Well, you're not having any more. So, finish your
coffee, wash your hands, then get into that dress.
Then come get your hair done before we go to
the church. And then, if Greg *ever* answers his
phone to confirm he's ready, hopefully we'll still
be on schedule.

RACHEL

Who's doing our hair?

JANE

On the day: a professional hairdresser. This
morning: mum's having a crack with the curling
tongs. Always have a backup plan.

JANE checks her MOBILE from BATHROBE pocket.

JANE

Especially when the groom never answers! You're
as bad as each other at getting ready. This is why
we have to practice everything!

RACHEL

He's probably slept in, or forgot or something ...

JANE

It's his big day too.

RACHEL

There's no denying it's becoming a very big day.

JANE

Try the dress.

RACHEL

I hate the dress.

JANE

Then just get drunk like normal so you don't care
what you're wearing. Or doing.

JANE makes to leave, then stops.

JANE

Though we definitely do not want a repeat of the Hen's Night.

RACHEL

I thought he was the stripper.

JANE

Just remember, Cousin Geoff wants to meet my fun, wonderful, gorgeous friend.

RACHEL

So, just be myself.

JANE wavers, trying to find a tactful phrasing.

JANE

Just try your best.

JANE departs.

GREG springs up and joins RACHEL, taking COFFEE to sip intermittently.

GREG

So, what happened at the Hen's Night? And who's this Geoff?

RACHEL

Never you mind! What do you mean by 'Until you proposed'?

GREG

She changed, like, instantly. Before, she was great.
Adorable. Sexy. Perfect. Everything I could want.

RACHEL

(Gritted teeth) Great.

GREG

And the sex. What I could tell you about the sex!

RACHEL

Please don't tell me anything about the sex.

GREG

I should. Just for context.

RACHEL

I can join the dots.

GREG

So did we. But then I got over-excited and
popped it way too soon.

RACHEL

(Raises "stop" hand) Details, Greg.

GREG

Popped the question.

RACHEL

Seriously, goldfish put more thought into their
actions than you do.

GREG

I might've finished your coffee.

RACHEL

I'm awake anyway.

GREG

Ever since then, she's been trying to change me.

GREG fetches TOAST from floor, considers eating it. RACHEL rushes over and snatches it from him.

RACHEL

Can't say I blame her.

RACHEL takes COFFEE and puts TOAST and COFFEE aside upon nearest available surface.

GREG

But this is, like, *totally*. Everything about me.

RACHEL

Of course she is. It's the one big compensation we get for being in a relationship.

GREG

Why?

RACHEL

A boyfriend is like buying a house. You don't get it for what it is, but for what it could be.

RACHEL motions towards an imaginary house before them.

RACHEL

A little paint here, nicer carpet, change the fittings. Next thing, you're knocking down walls and putting in a new kitchen.

RACHEL looks GREG up and down.

RACHEL

And face it Greg, you're what's known as a "Renovator's Dream".

GREG

But if the guy's not up to scratch to start with, why go out with him?

RACHEL

Because otherwise some of you might never date again. It's no reason to run out on her, though.

GREG

That's not all. The whole wedding thing, she's gone nuts.

RACHEL

She was nuts about them before you proposed.

GREG

This is like … *(Emphatic hand gestures)* … really nuts. Everything has to be perfect. I can't do perfect, it's too hard. You didn't do any of this trying to change me.

RACHEL

I barely knew you.

GREG

What would *you* do with me? Renovation-wise?

RACHEL

Burn you down for the insurance. She'll return to normal after the wedding. Eventually. Probably.

GREG

She also decided no sex until the big day.

RACHEL

And you agreed?

GREG

It's not something only half the couple can disagree. Why would she do something like that?

RACHEL

To make the honeymoon special? Abstinence makes the parts grow fonder? Give you time to read up and get better at it?

GREG

It can't be healthy. It's like rewrapping your Christmas presents and shoving them back up the chimney.

RACHEL

You managed to survive months when single.

GREG

That's because I *managed*. It's a bit difficult to *manage* when she's lying next to you most nights.

RACHEL

Can't you go manage in another room?

GREG

She's a cuddler. Move my arm and she wakes.

RACHEL

Use the other arm.

GREG

It's not the same. And it reminds me of an ex. Awful technique.

RACHEL

Can't you manage when she's out?

GREG

She's with me or rings constantly these days.

RACHEL

Just think how great the wedding night will be.

GREG

I can't last that long! I'm a time bomb.

RACHEL

Well, you're not exploding in here. Talk to her. Tell her about your doubts.

GREG

Are you nuts? I'm not going out there. She's scary enough, let alone with her mum.

RACHEL

She's not nuts, she's just excited.

A staccato knock on DOOR. GREG instantly darts behind DOOR.

RACHEL

Yes?

JANE enters swiftly with a SPOON containing some food. GREG holds DOOR in place to hide behind.

JANE

Here, taste.

RACHEL

Taste what?

JANE

Mouth. Open.

RACHEL opens mouth and JANE sticks in SPOON.

JANE

Taste.

RACHEL samples food. JANE removes SPOON.

JANE

Thoughts?

Mouth full, RACHEL ruminates then gives non-committal shrug.

JANE leans back to DOOR and shouts out.

JANE

(*Shouting*) She hates it, Mum. Throw it out and start again.

JANE holds SPOON at RACHEL's mouth.

JANE

Spit. Don't swallow.

RACHEL looks at JANE.

JANE

Calories. (*Nods at BRIDESMAID DRESS*) Dress.

RACHEL

Too late. Sorry.

JANE rolls her eyes then departs, closing DOOR.

GREG unfreezes in hiding spot, points after JANE.

GREG

And that's another thing ...

RACHEL

Okay. Maybe she's going a little nuts.

GREG

It's ridiculous. She even banned me from porn. I haven't looked at any for days … months.

RACHEL

Where's your phone?

GREG produces MOBILE from pocket, gives to RACHEL.

GREG

That's no good, the screen's too small to see what's going on.

RACHEL forces MOBILE back to him.

RACHEL

Ring her.

GREG

What?

RACHEL

I'll distract her so you can leave some cowardly voicemail that you need to talk. Not here, not now, and certainly not with me involved in any way.

GREG

I can't turn it on. She's been calling all morning. What if it goes off and I'm in here?

114

Seeing his point, RACHEL gives up in frustration. GREG puts MOBILE back in pocket.

RACHEL

You knew what you were getting yourself in for.

GREG

I didn't know she would be like this. You should have warned me.

RACHEL

Me?

GREG

You know her better.

RACHEL turns her back. GREG attempts his real agenda.

GREG

So, maybe if … *you* talked to her?

RACHEL instantly backs away.

RACHEL

Not a chance!

GREG

You're the expert.

RACHEL

No, I'm the housemate. Qualifying me only for splitting bills and sharing a bathroom without using all the hot water.

GREG

But you lived together. You have a bond, shared intimate secrets.

RACHEL

A kitchen, a couch, and a toilet seat—that's all we share. Anything else isn't my business. Particularly anything to do with you.

GREG

I knew you'd been avoiding me.

RACHEL wavers for a moment.

RACHEL

If there's any sharing, it's between you two. Lives together. Married. Forever. Don't come to me for advice on that, I'm the last person to know.

RACHEL sits on BED.

RACHEL

I thought things were going great for you two. You were keen on her dad. And his brewery.

GREG

Too yeasty.

RACHEL

Him or the beer?

GREG

Both, to be honest. His entire range is awful. And

he keeps feeding them to me when we visit.

RACHEL

You could say always no.

GREG

To a beer? He'll think I'm weird.

RACHEL

He'll have worked that out already.

GREG

I just thought you've been around a bit, clocked a few miles. You know how to phrase things. And you've broken at least one marriage already.

GREG produces NOTE from his JEANS pocket.

GREG

I came up with some reasons if you get short of ideas.

RACHEL takes NOTE, reads incredulously at the content.

GREG

Just email how it went when you're done.

RACHEL

I'm not doing it.

RACHEL scrunches NOTE and throws it to floor. GREG— remember where it ends up!

GREG

Who else can I go to for advice?

RACHEL

Your mum? The celebrant? The postman?
Anyone but me. Ask your married mates.

GREG

I can't ask them.

RACHEL

Why not?

GREG

… because I might not have told them yet.

RACHEL

Aren't some of them your groomsmen?

GREG

… They're bound to agree when I ask them.

RACHEL

When you ask them? The wedding is in a
fortnight.

GREG

That's why I insisted on a morning ceremony. In
case they can't get out of footy that arvo.

RACHEL

They're playing football on your wedding day?

GREG

Only if selected. The coach is pretty picky.

RACHEL

Jane thinks you have a full complement of groomsmen organised.

GREG

It's fine. They'll turn up anywhere for free beer. Even Jane's dad's mucky stuff.

RACHEL

(Grits teeth) Why haven't you told them you're getting married?

GREG

Because then they'll give me a buck's night. Which scares the absolute shit out of me.

RACHEL

Tell them you don't want one.

GREG

Every guy has a buck's night. And every single one is a near fatal drinking expedition to totally humiliate the groom.

RACHEL

Why would your friends do that to you?

GREG

In revenge for all the humiliating things I've done to them on their buck's nights.

RACHEL

Why did you do that?

GREG

(Shrugs) It's what you do on buck's nights.

RACHEL supresses rage at the circular logic.

RACHEL

What's the worst they could do?

GREG

Pretty much anything. We handcuffed Mick then shaved him bald *all* over. We handcuffed Paul to a flagpole—nude. We got Ian blind drunk then put him on a mystery flight—nude. And we handcuffed Sykesy then dropped him in a sack on the step of a nun's convent.

RACHEL

Nude?

GREG

We didn't stick around to see what they were wearing.

RACHEL

Your mate, not the nuns.

GREG

Oh yeah, he was nude.

RACHEL

What is it with males and aggressive drunken
nudity?

GREG

All I know is, it's winter and I don't want to be
handcuffed to anything—stationary, missionary
or otherwise.

RACHEL

So, on the big day, in front of both families,
there's a very real chance you'll have no
groomsmen at all, depending on footy fixtures.

GREG

Well, not necessarily both families ...

RACHEL stares in disbelief.

GREG

I told my parents to keep the weekend free. Just
with no specifics, in case I got cold feet. Pretty
wise call given the way things have panned out.

A knock on the DOOR. GREG and RACHEL react.

RACHEL

(Calls) Just a minute, I'm ... getting changed.

GREG steps back to watch her undress.

RACHEL urgently herds GREG backwards to BED.

GREG stops at the BED edge. They stand face to face, quite close.

A beat.

RACHEL points for him to hide. GREG races to hide behind BED.

Another knock. RACHEL pretends to attend to her pyjamas.

RACHEL
I'm not decent!

BOB enters with SUITCASE.

BOB
That's all right, neither am I. Oh! There's a familiar face.

GREG's head pops up.

BOB
And there's another one. Oh ho! You two up to old tricks again, eh? Dirty devils.

RACHEL
(Loud whisper) The door!

BOB
What about it?

RACHEL
Close it!

BOB turns and closes DOOR.

BOB

Better?

RACHEL

Only if you were on the other side of it. Why are you here?

BOB

The hotty with the muffins said to talk to you about the room for rent.

RACHEL

The who? With the what?

BOB

You're advertising a room to let?

RACHEL

Yes.

BOB

I'm here to see it. Thought I recognised the place.

RACHEL

No. Way.

BOB

I meet all the criteria in the advert. Non-smoker, reliable, steady income, good sense of humour.

RACHEL

You're old enough to be my father.

BOB

That's a bit ageist!

GREG

It is a bit ageist.

RACHEL

Okay. You're ineligible due to being a dodgy old drunk with the ethical instincts of a wombat.

BOB

You didn't say that in the advert.

RACHEL

There wasn't space. Why are you looking for a place? You're married.

BOB

The missus left me. And took the house with her.

RACHEL

Because you were seeing your "one" on the side?

BOB

Who left town. And took her husband with her.

GREG

(Tuts) They change on you, don't they.

BOB

They most certainly do, my lad.

RACHEL rounds on GREG.

RACHEL

This is totally different. Bob was having an affair!

BOB

Only of the heart. ... And some other bits.

GREG

Until your wife found out and ended it?

BOB

Leaving me with just this battered old case containing all I own and an empty hole where love used to be. I shall spend my time in quiet contemplation of my mistakes and sins. And maybe catch up some DVD boxsets. A humbled, lonely man with but memories and regret as company. *(Points)* Ooh, I like the wallpaper.

RACHEL

(Guilty) It's not wallpaper.

BOB

Oh. *(Looks about)* This the room?

RACHEL

This is my bedroom.

BOB

Blimey, the advert didn't say anything about
bunking up.

BOB sets SUITCASE down then sits on BED, testing for comfort.

RACHEL

Jane's room is across the hallway.

BOB

So, we'll need to keep the noise down.

RACHEL

She's the one moving out.

GREG

Not necessarily.

RACHEL

Yes, she is. With you. Once you're married.

BOB

You're getting married again?

GREG

Well …

RACHEL

Yes, he is.

BOB strides to GREG, shakes GREG's limp hand.

BOB

Sounds like congratulations are in order then!
When's the happy day?

GREG

I may never have one of those again.

RACHEL

In a fortnight. He has a mild case of nerves
today, but nothing a good talk—or a firm kick—
won't fix.

BOB

Ah, the old cold feet, eh?

BOB lays arm over GREG's shoulder, leads him aside.

BOB

We all get them, you know. Only natural. Foolish
doubts, insecurities gnawing away, making you
think the strangest things. And you know the best
way to solve the problem?

GREG

How?

BOB

You *run*, my lad. While you can. Where there's
smoke, there's an arsonist of your dreams
wearing a wedding ring. Run. Before you end up
like me, living out of a suitcase.

RACHEL

Bob!

GREG

That decides it then. You break the news to her.

BOB

Me?

GREG

You deal with divorces every day.

BOB

I'm too busy with my own.

GREG claps BOB's shoulder.

GREG

She'll need a big strong shoulder to cry on.

BOB wipes the dandruff loosened by GREG's clapping his shoulder.

GREG

And so might her mum.

BOB

(Interested) ... the one with the muffins?

GREG

You noticed those too.

BOB shakes GREG's hand.

BOB

Deal.

RACHEL blocks BOB's path to DOOR.

RACHEL

I am not letting you do this.

BOB

If he's not keen, then it's for the best.

RACHEL

If he's not keen, then he's an idiot.

BOB

I sign off on so many couple's marriages. And sadly, a few years or months later I sign the end of those that should never have been. If there's real doubt, sometimes prevention is for the best.

RACHEL slowly nods in agreement to this logic.

RACHEL

I guess you're right. For the best.

RACHEL steps aside. BOB proceeds to DOOR.

RACHEL

So, I guess you won't be taking the room, then.

RACHEL raises SUITCASE for him to collect.

RACHEL

Because if they call it off, Jane won't move in with him and so won't be moving out of here.

BOB

… could I batch on the sofa for a while?

RACHEL

Oh-my-god-hell-no.

A moment's thought then BOB strides to GREG.

BOB

Of course, you shouldn't be too hasty.

GREG

You've changed your tune.

BOB

And so should you. The girl's lovely!

GREG

You haven't met her.

BOB

Are you doubting my professional opinion?

GREG

… No.

RACHEL

Yes!

BOB

There you go. Hop in, my son. Boots and all.

BOB gives friendly slap on GREG's back, then returns to RACHEL.

BOB

I'll just pop a look at the room, shall I?

RACHEL

Not now. Jane won't want some old bloke poking about in her bedroom.

GREG

She's not even keen on my old bloke nowadays.

BOB

When can I have a poke about then?

RACHEL

Ask Jane.

BOB nods then opens door and shouts down hall.

BOB

(Shouts) Jane!

GREG and RACHEL rush to drag him back.

JANE

(Shouts from afar) I'm doing my hair!

RACHEL closes door then rounds on BOB.

RACHEL

It is vitally important Jane doesn't find out Greg is in here with me.

BOB

Oh, yes? *(Jumps to lewd conclusion)* Oh yes?

BOB gives GREG an elbow nudge.

BOB

One last fling before the nuptials, eh?

RACHEL

No!

GREG wavers from answering.

RACHEL

Come back later and look at the room.

BOB

But my bus doesn't come past for ages yet. I'll go check the muffins instead.

RACHEL makes to object but takes BOB's departure as a win.

BOB takes his SUITCASE and departs, then leans back in DOOR.

BOB

A little privacy for you lovebirds?

BOB closes the DOOR.

RACHEL

How quickly could I get the locks changed?

GREG

Bob's given me the solution.

RACHEL

Is that solution you manning up and going through with today's practice run. Then, if your heart's still not in it, you confess to her before the wedding that you're an idiot, a coward, and wouldn't know the best thing you'd ever had if it bit you. And I hope she does bite you. Hard. With teeth. Gnah!

RACHEL gnashes at GREG, who steps back from her bite.

RACHEL

Now go, so I can try my dress and keep one thing on-track for Jane before you break her heart.

RACHEL takes BRIDESMAID DRESS from CLOTHES RACK. GREG recoils at the sight of it.

GREG

Christ, you're wearing *that*?

GREG takes BRIDESMAID DRESS incredulously.

GREG

Does she have it in for you or something?

RACHEL snatches BRIDESMAID DRESS back.

GREG

I can't be with someone who could inflict *that* on another human being.

RACHEL

Yes, it's horrible and will be torture to wear. But I will so Jane gets the wedding day she wants.

RACHEL drops BRIDESMAID DRESS on BED.

GREG

Or maybe there are more selfish motives going on with this wedding?

RACHEL

You think *I'm* being selfish here?

GREG

Maybe someone is more concerned about their opportunity with Cousin Geoff than helping her friends from a terrible mistake?

RACHEL

You are not a friend, Greg. You're a speed bump on the pot-holed, wrong-way-go-back roadkill highway of my love life. It's literally a blind date. Besides, why can't I have an opportunity with someone?

GREG

You deserve better.

RACHEL

You haven't met him. *I* haven't met him.

GREG

Exactly. He's probably a knob.

RACHEL

Maybe. But since "better" isn't knocking down
my door—or pretending to be out when I knock
on theirs—I'm open to possibilities.

GREG

You weren't open to my possibilities.

RACHEL

Your possibilities ran off with my housemate in
front of me.

GREG

My possibilities were hardly left with a choice
after your possibilities shunned them.

RACHEL

Your possibilities didn't look too put out once
they caught sight of Jane's possibilities. My
possibilities didn't even get a look in!

GREG

… possibly.

RACHEL

You don't need possibilities, you have Jane.

GREG

But she's crazy.

GREG picks up BRIDESMAID DRESS, makes crazy noise.

RACHEL

No, she's not. It's you, building some idea in your head of Jane as some Bridezilla monster when she's nothing of the sort.

JANE enters, looking like Medusa with HAIR CURLERS, tending to huge false EYELASHES.

GREG immediately hides behind BRIDESMAID DRESS, RACHEL holds it up to conceal him.

JANE

What did you want? I'm doing my hair.

RACHEL

… just wanted to know when the bathroom would be free.

JANE

I knew you'd be in a big rush once you finally started getting ready. *(Squints)* Are you getting ready? *(Adjusts EYELASHES)* Why do people wear these? It's like being attacked by caterpillars.

RACHEL

No! Keep them on. You look … gorgeous.

136

JANE wavers then turns to depart.

JANE

Give me five more minutes to finish my curlers.

*JANE turns to go then turns back. RACHEL resumes holding
BRIDESMAID DRESS awkwardly to block view of GREG.*

JANE

And you really need to stop inviting strange old
men into our house. At the very least, that
particular one out there. He's offered to give
Mum a hand with her dumplings.

RACHEL

Bob will be leaving very soon.

JANE

I think he's chatting her up.

RACHEL

Tell him she's married, that'll put him off. Maybe.

JANE

She's flirting back! I've not told you, but things
are tense between Mum and Dad. Separate
rooms, hardly talking. And … *(Steadying breath)*
Dad's taken up golf.

RACHEL

I'll definitely tell him to stop right away.

JANE

That won't work, he's just bought a set of clubs.

RACHEL

You do your hair. I'll scare Bob away.

JANE

And he asked how many outlets I had.

RACHEL

Pardon?

JANE

Electrical power outlets, in my room.

RACHEL

How many power outlets are there in your room?

JANE stops to think. RACHEL's arms are tiring.

JANE

I dunno. Two. Three. Five? Shit, now that's going to bug me if I don't find out. I haven't got time for this today!

JANE turns to depart but can barely see due to EYELASHES.

JANE

I have no idea where the door is.

JANE feels for DOOR, finds the handle, then exits, cursing.

JANE

Frickin' caterpillars!

RACHEL angrily thrusts BRIDESMAID DRESS into GREG.

Flinching at its ugliness, GREG tosses it back to RACHEL.

RACHEL flings BRIDESMAID DRESS aside to floor.

Guilty, RACHEL picks up BRIDESMAID DRESS, dusts it off.

RACHEL

Will you please go!

GREG

I tell you, Bob is onto something.

RACHEL

Yes, Jane's mum from the sound of things.

GREG approaches RACHEL purposefully.

GREG

If Jane was to find us together. In your room.

*RACHEL backs, holding BRIDESMAID DRESS as deterrent.
GREG slowly advances as he talks.*

GREG

Totally plausible, after what happened between
us. Maybe a lingering spark, still there. Maybe it's

never gone away. Undiminished, despite what's happened since.

GREG nears. RACHEL's holds BRIDESMAID DRESS close as last barrier between their narrowing personal space.

GREG

And as much as we try to avoid each other, maybe it never will. Maybe all it took was the reality of a deadline, with no turning back, to realise a wrong decision was made.

GREG's hands join RACHEL's on BRIDESMAID DRESS.

GREG

And maybe now, one of us wonders what a mistake it was, things ending the way they did. That it ended at all. That maybe the right person was there all the time. And it's taken something this serious to realise … and act on it.

BRIDESMAID DRESS drops to floor between them.

A beat.

GREG

And as for me, well, I'm pretty easy at the best of times.

RACHEL pulls away, frustrated.

RACHEL

For crying out loud!

GREG

Jane would call the whole thing off.

RACHEL snatches BRIDESMAID DRESS, throws it on BED.

RACHEL

I don't blame her. It wouldn't work anyway. She trusts me.

GREG

It would if we were naked.

GREG begins peeling off SHIRT.

RACHEL

Whoah! Put that back on.

GREG

It's the only way, Rachel. This marriage is a major mistake.

RACHEL

Take off any more and you'll know exactly about major mistakes.

GREG kicks off his SHOES.

GREG

You know Jane will never break up with a catch

like me. Get 'em off.

RACHEL

I'm not doing that to Jane. She's my friend.

GREG

Exactly. Treachery with a friend makes it all the more final! Just tell her later that nothing happened and it was just a misunderstanding.

RACHEL

In what way is you standing naked in my bedroom "just a misunderstanding"?

GREG

You're right. In bed together would be much more realistic.

GREG unbuckles JEANS on the way to BED.

RACHEL

No way!

GREG

Nothing you haven't seen before.

GREG begins lowering JEANS seductively.

GREG

In fact, ... nothing you haven't—

BOB enters with PLATE of "cheesy nibbles". He has FLOUR on his cheeks. And flour handprints on his bottom if wardrobe permits.

BOB

Cheesy nibble anyone?

GREG instantly pulls JEANS back up.

RACHEL

No thanks, just avoided one. Door!

BOB closes DOOR.

BOB

Not interrupting anything am I?

GREG

Just the person I need!

BOB looks behind himself as GREG approaches.

GREG

I need you to go out there and in five minutes tell Jane to come in.

BOB

But she'll see you.

GREG

Exactly!

RACHEL

Spare room in jeopardy if you do.

143

GREG

Best mate in jeopardy if you don't.

BOB *is torn by indecision.*

GREG

Of course, if Jane doesn't move in, there'd actually be a vacancy at my place.

BOB

A vacancy?

GREG

Maybe a better fit. Two blokes—*mates*—living the bachelor life. Doing what we want, watching what we want, eating what we want. Not quite so free and easy here, from what Jane tells me.

RACHEL

What has Jane told you?

GREG

Temper tantrums, nagging about cleaning, fights over what's whose in the fridge.

RACHEL

She doesn't! ... does she? The bitch.

GREG

Whereas my place... if you scratch my back.

BOB *takes a step back.*

GREG

Meaning, you help me out now.

RACHEL

Bob, no.

GREG

Shush now, Josephine Stalin. Your reign of tyranny is nearing an end.

BOB

And it's a similar size room?

GREG

… not an actual room as such. But certainly well-appointed, with easy access, and great airflow.

RACHEL

It's the living room sofa, isn't it.

GREG

Yes, but it does extend into a bed. If we get a few milk crates. And some planks.

BOB

Well, they're easily picked up.

GREG

Exactly. You're in?

GREG offers hand to shake.

RACHEL steps in, unable to believe she is negotiating.

RACHEL

What if I was to offer some sweeteners?

BOB

(Wary) I don't take sugar. I'm sweet enough as is.

RACHEL

I mean, allowances. Privileges.

BOB

I'm listening.

RACHEL

First call on the television remote.

BOB

… and?

RACHEL

I'll do the dishes for the first month.

BOB

… still listening.

RACHEL

And Sunday morning pancakes.

BOB

Just to keep Jane from coming in here?

RACHEL nods in defeat.

GREG

Don't believe her lies, Bob. Jane says she can't be trusted.

BOB

Sorry, my lad. Airflow or not, I require the privacy only an actual room can provide.

BOB takes GREG aside.

BOB

Why don't you try a nice goodbye letter? The Dear John approach. Some say it's impersonal—insulting even. But it allows you to find just the right words for the impossible emotional chasm that's grown between you. What's more, you save yourself a stamp if you pop it in the letterbox on your way out.

GREG

(To RACHEL) I could email it for you to bung out on your printer.

RACHEL

That's Jane's!

GREG

In two weeks, what's hers is mine.

RACHEL

Not if you don't marry her! You can't send a break-up letter using the person's own printer. That's rubbing salt into the wounds. And uses up her print toner.

BOB lifts PLATE.

BOB

And that's exactly what these are needing.

RACHEL

Printer toner?

BOB

No. More salt. Now, if you'll excuse me, there are some sweet buns I promised to have a nibble at.

BOB departs with PLATE.

GREG resumes undoing his JEANS.

GREG

You're right. A letter will never work. We go with my original idea.

GREG drops his JEANS.

RACHEL

Put those back on!

GREG

It's for the greater good.

RACHEL

Yours, no one else's!

GREG

Do you really think Jane could ever truly be happy with me, long term? Sexual gratification-wise excepted, obviously.

RACHEL

Of course not.

GREG

Exactly. We're doing her a favour.

GREG hops into BED then wriggles under SHEET.

RACHEL

You better not be getting naked under there!

GREG discovers a sudden sensual pleasure.

GREG

Ooh. *Soft* sheets.

RACHEL

Cut that out and put your clothes back on!

GREG produces UNDIES, aims them like a slingshot on his fingers.

GREG

I mean it. I'll fire if you don't get in too.

RACHEL

You wouldn't dare.

GREG

I warn you—it's been a long hot week.

RACHEL dodges side to side, GREG following her every move.

GREG

Don't make me do it. We're better than this.

RACHEL stands defiantly.

GREG lets UNDIES fly. RACHEL gives a shriek.

GREG

Great idea! *(Sexual throes)* Oh! Oh!

RACHEL

No no no!

GREG

Oh yes yes!

RACHEL

Don't!

GREG

Don't stop!

RACHEL

Cut it out!

A knock on the DOOR. JANE calls from outside.

JANE

Are you all right in there?

RACHEL looks to GREG, who lifts sheet welcomingly.

RACHEL rushes to hold DOOR as JANE begins to open it.

RACHEL

Just trying on the dress. It's a bit tight.

JANE

I knew it! You totally scoffed that pizza last week.

RACHEL stands indignantly.

RACHEL

I did not!

JANE resumes opening DOOR. RACHEL blocks her progress.

JANE

Where's it tight? Chest, waist or just your bum?

GREG

(Prompting) Your bum.

RACHEL

(Automatically) The bum.

RACHEL glares at GREG then waves to hide. GREG refuses.

JANE

I did tell the seamstress to add some give for you.

RACHEL wants to protest but waves more emphatically at GREG.

GREG rolls his eyes then rolls off BED in SHEET.

RACHEL lets JANE in, who looks at RACHEL then BRIDESMAID DRESS on BED.

JANE

You haven't even got it on.

RACHEL

... I didn't want to crease it.

JANE

(Aghast) Did you crease it? *(Sighs)* You'll have to swap with Fleur. She's only coming for the buffet anyway.

RACHEL

It'll fit. I'll have stressed the weight off by then.

RACHEL anxiously checks GREG is still hiding.

JANE

Getting nervous about meeting Cousin Geoff?

RACHEL

Yeah, sure.

JANE

He'll love you. You're funny, pretty, and almost the spitting image of his first wife.

RACHEL

His what?

JANE

Oh. I didn't mention he used to be married? Big mistake. All three of them.

RACHEL

Three broken marriages is a *lot* of baggage.

JANE

Something you both have in common already!

RACHEL

Mine was annulled.

JANE

(Shrugs) Hand luggage then. Don't worry. Yer gonna git yerself a man! Oh, and eighteen.

RACHEL

Eighteen what?

JANE

Power outlets in my room. You asked.

RACHEL

Yes, but that was … hang on, *eighteen?*

JANE

It seems a lot.

RACHEL

What are you running in there? A meth lab?

JANE

The previous tenants were pretty shifty. *(Moves to DOOR)* Now, stay in here. We're letting the budgie out.

RACHEL

What budgie?

JANE

Aunty Beryl's. She loaned him so we could practice letting the doves loose after the exchange of vows.

RACHEL

You're letting doves loose *inside* a church?

JANE

So romantic! There won't be a dry eye in the house.

RACHEL

Or heads and shoulders if the doves panic. Why are you practicing with a budgie?

JANE

Do you know how much doves cost?

RACHEL

Dead or alive?

JANE

Lots. So, we're practicing with Basil today.
Luckily, Bob says he's an expert at handling birds.
But he startles really easily so we're keeping him
to the dining room for now.

RACHEL

Bob?

JANE

No, Basil. So, don't come out. And stop making
weird noises in here. You'll make him nervous.

RACHEL

Basil?

JANE

No, Bob. Mum said she'd kill him if anything
happens to Basil so he's a bit on edge. Aunt Beryl
adores him.

RACHEL

Bob?

JANE

No, Basil. Aunt Beryl hasn't even met Bob.

RACHEL

I'd keep it that way.

JANE

Fair point.

JANE departs. RACHEL closes DOOR, making sure she's gone.

GREG climbs back onto BED in SHEET.

RACHEL

You. Out, now.

GREG

What, in the buff?

RACHEL

Put your clothes back on.

GREG

Okay. Pass my undies.

RACHEL reaches for UNDIES but stops, realising her peril.

RACHEL

Get them yourself.

GREG

I'm comfortable here.

RACHEL

I'm not.

GREG

You'd prefer Jane see me sneaking out of your

bedroom naked. Actually, that's perfect!

GREG begins to rise from BED in SHEET.

RACHEL

You stay right there!

GREG

Make up your mind!

GREG lazes back contentedly.

GREG

Don't worry. Jane will only hate you a little while until eventually believing you it was all a big misunderstanding. We'll all laugh in the long run.

RACHEL

Jane would never forgive me. *I* would never forgive me.

GREG

I'll forgive you.

RACHEL

I'll never forgive you.

GREG

You come up with a better plan then.

RACHEL

Go talk to Jane. Not naked. Tell her how you feel. Then either agree to defer it, end it, or *anything* that doesn't involve me.

GREG

That sounds *completely* nuts. Tears and hurt all round. My way is much easier and efficient.

RACHEL

It's even easier and more efficient if I just told Jane what you're up to.

GREG

But then all her anger gets directed solely at me, like, forever. She'll hold so much anger and bitterness for such a long time. It'll ruin her. Better to spread it across the two of us.

RACHEL

Just talk. It's what mature couples do.

GREG

She'll only talk me back into it.

RACHEL

Are you really that weak-willed?

GREG

Have you ever argued with her?

RACHEL

Yes.

GREG

Ever win?

RACHEL

I should wish.

GREG

See!

RACHEL

Go, now. Be a man. Sort this out.

RACHEL opens DOOR for GREG to leave.

SOUND FX: Bird tweeting, clattering silverware, furniture scrapes.

BOB

(OFF) Come back here you little bastard!

RACHEL closes DOOR, weary of life's misfortunes.

GREG

New plan?

GREG rises from BED, still wrapped in SHEET, thinking.

GREG

You need to put her off me. Make her see I'm not worth marrying.

RACHEL

That's hardly mission impossible.

GREG

Get her talking, then start seeding subtle doubts.

RACHEL

By bagging you out? I could plant a forest.

GREG

Bring up how marriage is such a *big* commitment. Is this *really* what she wants. The way you usually bring people down about things.

RACHEL

Maybe I just remind her you're a dickhead and ask what the hell she's thinking?

GREG

She'll hardly fall for that. You need to really sway her opinion. When she mentions my great points, you make up something negative. Do you need my list of suggestions?

RACHEL

No, no. I'm good.

GREG shuffles to wherever NOTE ended up.

GREG

Because I jotted down some plausible ideas you could use.

RACHEL

No, I've got heaps.

GREG

(Confused then shrugs) Okay. So, get her looking for those red flags, then whumpo! She'll call it all off

in no time.

RACHEL

So, basically, I prime her to notice you treating her like crap?

GREG

Only now I'll be doing it deliberately, as opposed to natural unawareness.

RACHEL

That is the most manipulative thing I have ever heard.

GREG

It's the only way to avoid breaking her heart. Her eyes opened by her best friend. You'll be a *hero*.

RACHEL

It's totally deceitful.

GREG returns to BED.

GREG

A lesser evil for a greater good, and the warm glow from helping two friends avoid a terrible mistake. *And* having Bob as a housemate. And hey, I'll be back on the market.

RACHEL

So?

GREG assumes provocative posture in BED.

GREG

Just putting it out there.

RACHEL

You can put it straight back in again.

GREG raises his eyebrows.

RACHEL

Not like that.

GREG

You know, it's okay for us to admit to buyer's remorse with the way things turned out.

RACHEL

I didn't buy anything. I was dumped at the store for a refund.

GREG

Do you ever think about what could have been? What we could have been?

RACHEL

No.

GREG

I mean, *really.*

RACHEL

Yes.

GREG

Yes?

RACHEL

Yes. I *really* mean no.

GREG

So, no chance of still holding a little candle for
the other?

RACHEL

You can hold your little candle all you want. Not
a day goes by I don't regret everything with you.

GREG

That it happened, or that it ended?

RACHEL wavers, then marches to DOOR, opens and calls out.

RACHEL

(Calls) Jane, can you come here, please. I need to
tell you something.

GREG

Thanks a million, Rach.

GREG relaxes. RACHEL waits, then realises.

RACHEL

Well, hide then!

GREG ducks under the sheet.

RACHEL

That's no good.

Still covered in SHEET, GREG sits up, looks about, then flings himself off BED still wrapped in SHEET ...

... as JANE enters, stressed. RACHEL acts casual.

JANE

I'm really busy, Rachel. We're due at the church soon, Greg still isn't answering his phone, and Basil won't come down from the ceiling fan. *(Realises)* And you *still* haven't tried on your dress!

RACHEL

Let's take a breath and calm it down.

JANE

I haven't got time!

RACHEL leads JANE by hand to BED.

RACHEL

We'll make time.

RACHEL sits JANE on BED with her back to where GREG is hiding. RACHEL calmly sits on BED.

RACHEL

So, how are things looking?

JANE immediately stands.

JANE

It. Is. Chaos! Have you *ever* tried planning a
wedding? *(Realises)* Oh. Sorry.

JANE sits and pats RACHEL's leg sympathetically.

JANE

Never mind. One day. Probably.

RACHEL

(Gritted teeth) Thank you.

JANE

Maybe if you and Cousin Geoff hit it off. He's
quite a spunk now he's lost some of his weight.

RACHEL

Some?

GREG pops up, grinning. RACHEL leans back, waves him down.

JANE produces her MOBILE.

JANE

He asked for more pictures of you. Hope you
don't mind.

RACHEL

Only if you sent good ones.

JANE shows MOBILE to RACHEL.

JANE

The photos from Monica's pool party.

RACHEL

I'm wearing an enormous hat and sunglasses.

JANE

That's okay, he only wanted ones in a bikini.

JANE puts MOBILE away.

RACHEL

... right. *(Plows on)* Anyway, about the big day.

JANE

Big is not the word. Two hundred people now.

RACHEL

Oh my ...

JANE

And that's just my family. Who knows how many will eventually RSVP on Greg's side.

GREG floats up to shrug. RACHEL glares.

JANE

Dad's costing for three hundred, give or take.

RACHEL

He hasn't paid a bond yet, has he?

JANE

Upfront in cash. You know my dad. Hates a debt.

RACHEL

Oh great.

JANE

Exactly. It's all going to be great.

RACHEL

Including Greg?

JANE

Yeah, he's grea- … He's a good man.

RACHEL

Sure. A *good* man.

Dissatisfied with efforts so far, GREG bobs up to wave NOTE. RACHEL leans back and shoos him.

RACHEL

Pretty good. Reasonably. But not *great*.

JANE

You shouldn't expect perfection. I've always said that. And not just to cheer you up.

RACHEL

You don't think you could maybe do a *bit* better?

JANE

I can make Greg better. Clothes, haircut. Wash a

bit more. Mould him like putty into perfect.

GREG rises, pointing, his suspicions proved. RACHEL discreetly shoos him down again.

RACHEL

But there's only so much you can do with putty.

JANE

True. I was pretty shit at pottery in high school. I got detention just for making a fruit bowl.

RACHEL

Why?

JANE

My teacher thought I'd made a sex toy.

RACHEL

That's a pretty bad fruit bowl.

JANE

I know. It only held two bananas.

RACHEL

But otherwise, things are okay? No last-minute jitters? No fears it's all a *terrible* mistake?

Making a deduction, JANE pats RACHEL's leg.

JANE

Just because things ended so badly for you, doesn't mean Greg and I are making the same awful embarrassing mistakes.

RACHEL
Thanks.

JANE
I know it's awkward, me sort of stealing Greg from you.

RACHEL
Only in the way someone steals a dose of measles.

JANE
I get that you feel jealous. Given your luck with relationships—those that actually made it that far—I see how you became so bitterly cynical.

RACHEL
I'm just waiting for the right guy to come along.

JANE
And it's great you use that to convince yourself nothing's wrong.

JANE gives RACHEL a hug. RACHEL pushes onwards.

RACHEL
But are you happy to go through with it? Really?

JANE
It's my wedding day—how could I not be?

RACHEL

Because you're marrying *Greg*. You don't think the reason you're working so hard to make the wedding perfect is because you're compensating for a groom that isn't?

GREG pops up to acknowledge a point well made.

JANE

It's like going to a cafe that serves really good chocolate mud cake. *Really* good, every single time. Then one day, their chef leaves, taking the recipe with them. The last slice is already gone. No more chocolate mud cake.

RACHEL and JANE look longingly into the distance.

JANE

So, they offer you a banana sundae instead, with a flake stuck in the side, free of charge.

RACHEL and JANE react to this unsatisfying substitute.

JANE

And it's nice and all. Does the job, fills a spot. But it's not the chocolate mud cake.

RACHEL continues staring into the distance, yearningly.

RACHEL

I'd like some chocolate mud cake one day.

JANE

You don't fit your bridesmaid dress already.

RACHEL glares at JANE, the spell broken.

JANE

And really, that's Greg what is.

RACHEL

The flake on the side?

GREG rises to protest, RACHEL leans back, points him down.

JANE

(Sighs) Greg isn't the man of my dreams.
Especially the dreams I have, particularly when
I've eaten zucchini. No, my chocolate cake was
always James.

RACHEL

James?

GREG pops up, mouthing "James?". RACHEL shrugs.

JANE

He lived on my street. We played all the time
together as kids. He said I was the only girl who
didn't smell of dog farts.

RACHEL

That's still probably a more solid basis for
marriage than Greg.

GREG sinks back down, not happy with the conversation.

JANE

He proposed to me. Year one, standing in line for the tuckshop. Down on one knee. Though he might've been looking at a centipede. Proposed again in year two, and year three. At least twice in year four. Most Wednesdays in year five. He lost interest in year six, only one proposal per term— he got a mountain bike the previous Christmas, so that's to be expected. Then he moved away.

RACHEL

What a shame he fell out of contact.

JANE

Yeah. From then on, he only wrote letters every few weeks. And poems about me. Then once he got email it was every second day. SMSs when he got a phone. Webcam chats. Sketches he drew instead of studying at college. And such lovely wistful songs about unrequited love.

RACHEL

But you eventually drifted apart?

JANE

Pretty much. Except for visits on school breaks, when he'd tell me how he didn't like any of the girls at college. That he could never find one that could measure up to me.

RACHEL

... wow.

JANE

I know. All the best guys are always gay.

RACHEL

He's gay?

JANE

Well, he has girlfriends now and then—models, mostly. Just for show, because he says they mean nothing compared to me. Always asks if I'm seeing anyone, as if he needs more drama and gossip in his life!

RACHEL

And you've never done anything about this?

JANE

Of course I do. I wish him well every Mardi Gras and ask him for hair and skincare tips.

RACHEL

And what does he say?

JANE

Usually just goes quiet for a while. Or gets a bit sniffy. Hayfever probably. Or cocaine. You know those gay guys!

RACHEL

Jane, he's not gay.

JANE

Of course he is. It's obvious.

RACHEL

He's madly in love with you, and you keep pushing him away because … you're *insane*. Is he coming to the wedding?

JANE

He said he was busy doing his hair. Or some other guy's if you ask me.

RACHEL

He's not gay, he's heartbroken! He's wanted you all his life and you keep knocking him back on some fundamentally strange assumption he's homosexual. Then invite him to your wedding to someone who's basically a sloth with a day job!

GREG bobs up to protest, realises she has a point, sinks down again.

RACHEL

Did he say anything else?

JANE

Nothing. Except that if I ever changed my mind, he'd be here on the next plane, car, or speedboat to take me away. Where do gay guys get the money for all these thrill-seeker holidays?

RACHEL stands, lifting JANE then shaking her by the shoulders.

RACHEL

Ring him. Now.

JANE

But I need to ring the photographer.

RACHEL

(Pushing JANE to DOOR) Stuff the photographer. Ring James immediately!

JANE

Okay. But I think you're totally misreading things.

JANE departs. GREG stands, shocked.

GREG

I can't believe it.

RACHEL

Am I good or am I good?

GREG

Never mind that. This James guy has been totally chasing my fiancée behind my back.

RACHEL

The fiancée you're cowardly dropping.

GREG

But the indiscretion! It goes totally against The Guy Code.

RACHEL

This is exactly what you wanted!

GREG

Not like this! With some guy totally white anting me to steal Jane. That sort of behaviour can't be rewarded.

RACHEL

You're naked in my bedroom, coercing me with your undies to jump into bed with you.

GREG

Only today. Not some continual, sneaky wearing-you-down, like this James bloke.

RACHEL

I've sorted it for you. You're saved.

GREG

Not by being cuckolded by some fancy peacock, prancing in to steal my girl. No way.

GREG shuffles in SHEET over to JEANS, searches for MOBILE.

GREG

I'm ringing Jane right now to win her back from this sneaky bugger then she can dump me properly, with my pride intact.

RACHEL

Greg, you can't cockblock true love. This guy is besotted with her. He's the love of her life!

GREG has hopefully produced his MOBILE by now.

GREG

I can, and I will!

BOB enters with SUITCASE.

BOB

I have, and I shall!

GREG switches on MOBILE, waits for it to boot.

RACHEL

Shall what?

BOB

Take the room. It's a squeeze, but I'm living out of a suitcase anyway.

RACHEL

Take your suitcase and buzz off.

BOB

That's not how to start with your new housemate.

RACHEL

You're not. I have to approve you.

BOB

Do you?

RACHEL

Yes.

BOB *takes RACHEL's hand and shakes.*

BOB

Good, that's settled then.

GREG

Welcome aboard, Bob.

RACHEL

That wasn't a yes.

GREG

Sounded like a yes to me.

BOB

That's settled then.

Holding SHEET, GREG struggles to operate MOBILE with one hand. Eventually, he uses his nose to press MOBILE screen.

BOB

Now, how do you feel about trumpets? Because I like to rehearse three times a week.

RACHEL

You are not bringing a trumpet in here.

BOB

(Taps SUITCASE) Already have. My doctor prescribed it as a hobby to distract from the wife leaving. I'm getting quite good at it. Almost totally mastered Three Blind Mice. Quite topical given the way we three met, eh?

RACHEL

No. *(To BOB)* No, to *you.*

RACHEL grabs GREG's MOBILE, shoves it into JEANS pocket, then forces JEANS upon him.

RACHEL

And especially no to you. You're not devastating Jane's life twice today by wrecking the best option she's ever had.

GREG

It's not twice today. One of the devastations will be later in the week.

BOB

Uh oh, trouble in paradise?

GREG

Another bloke is chasing Jane behind my back.

BOB

Disgraceful! You must be livid. Kick her out!

GREG

Exactly! I've should dump all her stuff back here right now.

GREG drops JEANS, shuffles angrily in SHEET to DOOR.

BOB

(Worried) Back into my new bedroom?

GREG

Yep!

BOB sets SUITCASE down and blocks GREG's way.

BOB

Win her back, mate. Are you a man or a mouse?

RACHEL

He's barely a hamster.

BOB

You can't let some bloke waltz in and steal your girl!

RACHEL

Yes, he does!

GREG

No, I don't.

BOB

You need to do something audacious. *(Idea)* Propose to her!

GREG

I already have.

BOB

Did it work?

GREG

Yeah, she was stoked.

BOB

There you go then. Problem solved.

RACHEL

So has the other guy. Almost every day since they were both six years old.

BOB

Did she say yes?

RACHEL

They were *six*.

BOB

She has doubts then. Ball's in your court, mate.

RACHEL

He doesn't want her balls!

BOB

This sounds a bit more complicated than I thought.

JANE

(Clarifies) In his court. Up until ten minutes ago, Jane's balls could go bounce for all he cared.

GREG

I care very much for those balls, thank you very much! But any ball movements from my court to anyone else's should be through the natural course of a match. Not some bloke suddenly running on and snatching them away. That's a code violation any way you choose to see it.

BOB

Especially if you were still bouncing them.

GREG

Sadly, we stopped bouncing them weeks ago.

RACHEL

Can we please stop talking balls. Jane's happiness is far more important than your fragile male ego.

BOB *raises his hand and steps forward.*

BOB

Amongst my varied duties as State Registrar are significant conflict mediation skills. What's needed here is all parties having a good sit down to clear the air on the key issues.

RACHEL

Exactly what I've been saying.

BOB

Namely, how we'll be splitting bills and a cleaning roster for the bathroom. I warn you now, I'm a particularly hairy man in a surprising number of places.

RACHEL

You are not moving in! *(To GREG)* And *you* are letting Jane be with someone truly who loves her.

RACHEL moves to DOOR.

RACHEL

Jane! Can you come here, please.

JANE

(OFF) I'm on the phone!

GREG shuffles in SHEET to confront RACHEL.

GREG

No way! These Chocolate Mud Cake guys always win out. It's not fair.

RACHEL

It's not about you, or him, it's about Jane.

GREG

And maybe a bit about you and Cousin Geoff.

RACHEL

This has nothing to do with Cousin Geoff!

BOB

Is it normally this busy here? I may be insisting on limiting houseguest numbers.

GREG

It's in your interest to marry Jane off one way or another to get your big chance to cop off with the wonderful Cousin Geoff. I bet he's another Mr Chocolate Mud Cake.

RACHEL

I haven't even met Cousin Geoff.

GREG

Making your manipulation all the more selfish.

BOB

He's got a point.

RACHEL

No, he hasn't.

BOB

(To GREG) Maybe you don't.

GREG

I think I have. Definitely touched a nerve.

RACHEL

The only nerve is yours, involving me in your schemes then making me feel bad about meeting someone. I may not even like Cousin Geoff.

GREG

I don't think you will.

RACHEL

Think or hope?

GREG

Both.

They stop, both surprised at this significant admission.

JANE shouts repeated "oh my god!" from OFF. GREG urgently shuffles/hops to hide behind BED. RACHEL and BOB move to block view of GREG.

JANE rushes in, holding BOUQUET and her MOBILE.

JANE

Oh my god. I rang James. You were right.

RACHEL

He isn't?

JANE

He's not!

RACHEL

Then is he ...?

JANE

He is!

RACHEL

Hang on, which is which.

JANE

He's coming straight here. And ... *straight*. He said to pack my things and wait out front for him.

RACHEL

Now?

JANE

He secretly came to town for one last try at

talking me out of the wedding. He'll be here in minutes, charging in on his gleaming white motorcycle. A Kawasaki Deus Ex Machina.

BOB

Blimey Charlie!

JANE

(Corrects) No, *Kawasaki.*

RACHEL

Don't just stand there, go pack!

JANE

But what about Greg? He'll be devastated.

RACHEL

I'll tell him. I've ended a marriage to him once already. It's easy with practice.

BOB

And his balls weren't bouncing anyway.

RACHEL elbows BOB in the ribs.

RACHEL

I'll phrase it somehow.

JANE

No. He needs to hear this from me.

JANE presses MOBILE and waits for answer.

SOUND FX: ROB'S MOBILE VIBRATING

JANE, RACHEL, BOB look to JEANS on floor—which might even move a bit with the magic of special effects.

GREG stands guiltily, clad in SHEET.

JANE

Greg. What are you doing here? In the nude.

GREG

I'm ... practising. For my buck's night.

JANE

In Rachel's bedroom?

GREG

... I thought she might have some handcuffs?

All eyes to RACHEL. She sighs, points to BEDSIDE CABINET.

RACHEL

Second drawer.

JANE looks accusingly to GREG, then RACHEL.

JANE

(Shrugs) Fair enough. *(Sombre)* Greg, I'm afraid I've something to tell you.

GREG immediately assumes stoic pose.

GREG

Do you?

JANE

I can't marry you.

GREG recoils, melodramatic clutch at his chest.

GREG

What? No!

JANE

There's someone else. In fact, there's always been someone else. I just didn't know, until now.

GREG covers face with forearm, as though in a Jane Austen novel.

GREG

Oh! That this should be true! The heartbreak!

JANE

I'm so sorry. Can you ever forgive me?

GREG holds hand in dramatic yearning, then bites finger in mock indecision, until finally serene.

GREG

I shall. If your heart be with another, I must not stand in your way. Free, free. I set you free. Go now, with my blessing.

JANE

I thought you'd be angry, but no. There's so much more to you than meets the eye.

GREG adjusts SHEET, fearing a gap.

JANE

May you find someone more worthy one day.

GREG humbly bows. RACHEL is unable to take any more.

RACHEL

Jane, seriously.

JANE

And I'm sorry for you, too. Wedding's off. For now, anyway. Oh no! Someone needs to break the news to Mum. She has two hundred vol-au-vents in the oven.

BOB steps forward.

BOB

Never fear. I shall be her rock-solid shoulder of comfort and sympathy. *(Brushes dandruff)* Plus, I can reheat them all for lunch this week.

JANE turns to RACHEL before leaving.

JANE

You were wrong about fairy tales. At least for me, with my perfect prince racing here on his throbbing white stallion. And you had your heart so set on Uncle Geoff.

RACHEL

I guess ... *Uncle*? You've been saying cousin.

JANE

I always think of him as my cousin. My much older cousin. And he pays me a fifty if I say it around my single friends.

RACHEL

You're matching me with your dirty old uncle? You said he was hunky.

JANE

I did. "Hunky" with a silent 'c' at the start. You said you no longer expected perfection in a man.

RACHEL

Perfection, not complete fabrication!

SOUND FX: A motor bike arrives, beeps horn.

JANE

Oh my god, it's James! Thanks for everything. Not sure when I'll be back. Don't wait up!

JANE passes BOUQUET to RACHEL.

JANE

In fairytales, it's meant to be the wicked witch who puts up all the thorns and spikes to keep the princes away, not the princess herself.

SOUND FX: *Another motorbike horn beep.*

JANE giggles then rushes out DOOR.

BOB

All's well that ends well. I'll move in Tuesday.

RACHEL

What?

BOB

Deal's a deal. I held my end of the bargain. I
wonder if my waterbed will fit.

BOB produces MEASURING TAPE, gives it a quick test.

GREG

What about Jane's mum?

BOB

All in good time, my lad. I might ask her help
with the dusting. See if we get way-hey-hay fever.

BOB pockets MEASURING TAPE, picks up SUITCASE.

BOB

But first, I must break the news to her and
provide solace. *(Idea)* Maybe she should have a
blow of my trumpet. *(Taps SUITCASE)*

BOB offers handshake to GREG.

BOB

Been a hard deal of the cards for you today, lad.
A right royal flush. Best of luck, my son.

Struggling with SHEET, GREG manages handshake.

BOB approaches RACHEL.

BOB

Spare key?

RACHEL

On the rack hanging in the kitchen.

*RACHEL gives BOUQUET to BOB. He gratefully accepts and
strides OUT with SUITCASE.*

SOUND FX: Motor bike departing.

GREG listens glumly.

GREG

There she goes. For the best. For Jane, anyway.

GREG returns to BED in SHEET.

RACHEL trudges to BED and cocoons herself with DOONA.

RACHEL

All for the best. For Jane, anyway.

SOUND FX: Trumpet blaring inept Three Blind Mice from outside.

RACHEL looks to DOOR.

SOUND FX: Trumpet squeaks as though player was interrupted.

RACHEL

I may have to get my room soundproofed. Or
just seal it airtight.

They lie still.

GREG

So, here we are again.

RACHEL

Here we are. Loveless and discarded.

A beat.

RACHEL

Are you still holding a candle for me?

GREG

… it's not impossible a flicker exists. Still.

RACHEL nods, taking this information in.

GREG

And you?

RACHEL

A candle to torture a voodoo doll of you over. …
But, a lit candle, I guess.

GREG nods, taking this information in.

GREG

Sometimes I rush in and make a mess of things.

RACHEL

You surprise me.

GREG

Then regret the decisions I didn't take.

RACHEL

(Defensive) Too late now, Jane's already left.

GREG

I mean decisions *overlooked.* That maybe my first
instinct was right. Before I ran off chasing all my
next first instincts.

RACHEL

Our first instincts were drunk irresponsible sex
and damn the consequences. And *damn*, those
consequences.

They nod glumly.

GREG

Would you like to … *date* for a bit?

RACHEL

Date?

GREG

Like new. Begin again. We had the marriage
annulled, maybe we could annul all the rest?

RACHEL

That's a very big ask.

GREG

It is. But I *am* asking.

RACHEL bites lip, unsure.

GREG

So. How about it?

Struck by these words, RACHEL looks at GREG then the DOOR.

RACHEL

(Wary) We would *have* to take things slow. No
marriage proposals for at least the first two years.

GREG

Years?

RACHEL

And sober. Totally sober, both of us.

A beat then GREG offers hand to shake.

GREG

Hi. I'm Greg. Renovator's Dream.

RACHEL

(Considers, then shakes) Rachel. Soft centre when you crack the surface.

SOUND FX: Trumpet squeal.

BOB chortling and female giggles can be heard OFF.

BOB

(OFF) Way-hey-hey!

GREG

Jane's mum was never like that at Sunday dinners.

RACHEL turns back to GREG, their hands still clasped.

GREG

So. Annulled, then?

RACHEL takes a decisive breath, shakes GREG's hand.

RACHEL

Let's consider those consequences cleared.

RACHEL frees her hand.

RACHEL

Meaning we're free to maybe damn a few new
ones ...?

RACHEL begins removing TOP, GREG pulls DOONA over them.

GREG

Daaamn!

LIGHTS DOWN.

END

Props List

ACT ONE:

- BED with SHEET and PILLOWS
- BEDSIDE TABLE with LAMP
- Rachel's MOBILE
- WINE GLASS
- DOONA
- DRESSER with MIRROR and CHAIR
- Greg's clothes (BOXERS, JEANS, SHIRT, SHOES)
- Rachel's KNICKERS
- Rachel's clothes (BRA, PYJAMA TOP and BOTTOMS)
- CLOTHES RACK
- CREDIT CARD (in Greg's JEANS pocket)
- BAR MAT (in Greg's JEANS pocket)
- CERTIFICATE (in Greg's JEANS pocket)
- SOFT TOY (on/near BED)
- TRAFFIC CONE(s) (under BED)
- GNOMES (under BED)
- Other random stolen items from a drunk walk home
- FRYPAN
- APRON

- Car KEYS
- PLATE with BACON

ACT TWO:

- Awful apricot baggy BRIDESMAID DRESS
- Jane's TOWEL and BATHROBE
- PLATE with TOAST and COFFEE MUG
- Jane's MOBILE
- SPOON
- Greg's MOBILE
- Greg's NOTE (in Greg's JEANS pocket)
- Bob's SUITCASE
- Hair CURLERS
- Huge false EYELASHES
- PLATE with "cheesy nibbles"
- FLOUR
- Male UNDIES with elastic slingshot capability
- BOUQUET of flowers
- MEASURING TAPE

Glossary

Doona—Australian word for padded blanket / duvet / quilt / bed cover, but only if officially sourced from the Doona region of Australia.

Cheezel—A brand of Australian cheese-flavoured snack, ring-shaped with a vaguely finger-sized hole. Lethal in some applications. Adapt to whatever local variation of circular snack.

Bra—Short for brassiere. Quicker to say, still difficult to unhook in a hurry.

Ugg boots—A boot made of sheepskin with the wool as the lining and the leather as the outside. Very snug and comfortable, except for the sheep involved. Usually indoors/bedtime wear, running away from anyone wearing them outdoors is suggested.

About the Author

Martin Lindsay is a Western Australian writer hidden away in the leafy seaside town of Dunsborough.

He is the author of the plays *Spd D8n*, *One Night One Day* and *Brown Acid*, and award-winning one-act plays *One Night Stand Off* and *Past Loves*.

Other plays include one-act *Someone Called Rob*, and finalists in the Short + Sweet and Arkfest ten-minute play festivals with *Couch*, *The Retirement Gift*, *That Little Voice*, and *Possum Play*.

Martin was a contributing writer for *Lifted* in the 2013 Perth Fringe Festival, and co-wrote and directed the comedy monologue/burlesque *Lock-In Love* for the 2014 Adelaide Fringe Festival and 2014 Melbourne Comedy Festival.

Martin's short stories have been included in Black Inc's *Best Australian Stories 2012*, and won the 2013 Stringybark Humorous Short Story Competition, the 2014 Joe O'Sullivan Writers Prize, and the 2019 Peter Cowan Short Story award. His micro-fiction has appeared in Short and Twisted editions and Night Parrot Press' *Once* (2020), *Twice Not Shy* (2021), and *Three Can Keep a Secret* (2022) collections.

He is even known to occasionally blog on his website at martinlindsay.net, when not trying to stop parrots from having sex on his balcony railing.

Martin's debut novel *Wil, Maree and the Mattress* will be available soon from Moody Lapcat Books.

Plays by the Same Author

- One Night One Morning

- Brown Acid

- Someone Called Rob

- Past Loves

- Couch

- Framed

- The Retirement Gift

- That Little Voice

- Possum Play

- Third Date's the Charm

Spd D8n

**A play in two acts by
Martin Lindsay**

Spd D8n

A play in two acts by
Martin Lindsay

At a speed dating evening at a local pub, five singles consider the question—How much can you really learn about someone in four minutes?

Ahead of them is a night of hope, hell, and free Cosmopolitans.

And maybe the chance to find what they didn't know they were looking for.

*"Hang on. I'm not **quite** drunk enough to make the end of your story."*

"How did you get into that line of work? Did you not study?"

"That possibly came across as a bit needy."

"Polyamory sounds an awful lot like just rootin' around."

"They call me Mike. Rhymes with bike. Maybe you can ride me sometime."

Available now from Moody Lapcat Books.

207

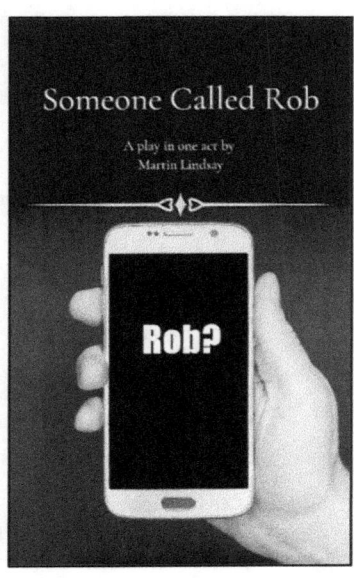

Someone Called Rob

**A play in one act by
Martin Lindsay**

Sometimes it pays to just let
the call go through to
voicemail ...

Rob answers an unknown caller on his mobile.

An angry guy called Adam reveals just what Rob did last
night. That's why Adam is angry.

And *everyone* knows what happens when Adam gets angry.

As Rob learns, a lot can be discovered from just a phone
number.

Available now from Moody Lapcat Books.

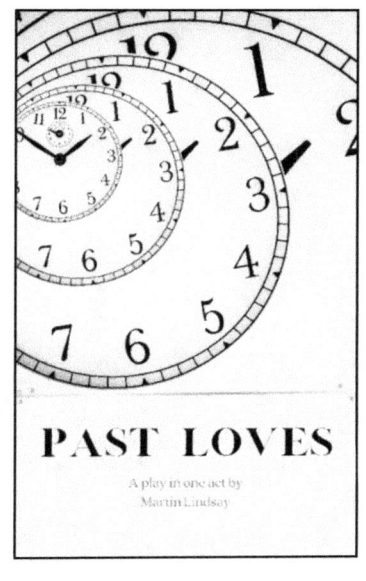

Past Loves

A play in one act by
Martin Lindsay

Ben is having a very good year. It just doesn't happen to be the current one.

Invited to coffee by his best mate's wife, Ben's life … lives … are about to be turned upside down.

And not just by the price of a latte these days.

'It happened before I could stop it. If I'd known where things would go.'

'Where did things go?'

'Where do you think things went!'

'I've heard a lot about <u>you</u>, Ben.'

'This will work much better with open minds.'

'If not completely vacant ones.'

Available now from Moody Lapcat Books.

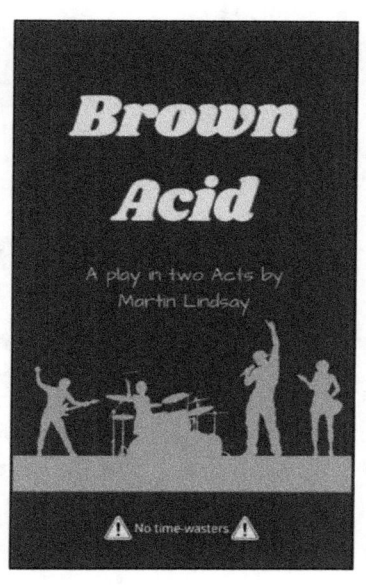

Brown Acid

A play in two acts by Martin Lindsay

Throughout rock'n'roll history, from small beginnings sometimes legendary bands grow ...

And sometimes, they don't.

Wanted:

Musicians to join original four-piece rock band.

Serious gigging opportunities with a group that is going places. Own transport would suit.

NO TIME WASTERS!

Coming soon from Moody Lapcat Books.

Moody Lapcat Books

Books better than belly rubs

Moody Lapcat Books is an independent publisher of books and plays.

Visit moodylapcatbooks.com to see our latest releases, things to come, or enquire about performance rights.

Or contact@moodylapcatbooks.com